KINGFISHER • TREASURIES

Ideal for reading aloud with younger children, or for more experienced readers to enjoy independently, Kingfisher *Treasuries* offer the very best writing for children. Carefully chosen by expert compilers, the content in each book is varied and wide-ranging. There are modern stories, traditional folk tales and fables, stories from a variety of cultures around the world, as well as work from exciting contemporary authors.

Popular with both children and their parents, books in the *Treasury* series provide a useful introduction to new authors and encourage children to take pleasure in reading.

KINGFISHER
Larousse Kingfisher Chambers Inc.
95 Madison Avenue
New York, New York 10016

First American edition 1996
2 4 6 8 10 9 7 5 3 1

LIBRARY OF CONGRESS CATALOGING-IN-PUBLICATION DATA

Kinder- und Hausmärchen. English. Selections
A treasury of stories from the Brothers Grimm / [compiled by]
Jenny Koralek : [illustrated by] Robin Lawrie.—1st American ed.
p. cm.
Summary: A collection of familiar fairy tales, including "The
Musicians of Bremen," "The Fisherman and His Wife," and
"Rumpelstiltskin."
1. Fairy tales—Germany.
[1. Fairy tales. 2. Folklore—Germany.]
I. Grimm, Jacob, 1785–1863. II. Grimm, Wilhelm, 1788–1859
III. Koralek, Jenny. IV. Lawrie, Robin, III.
PZ8.K57Tr 1996
398.2'0943'01—dc20 95-41101 CIP AC

ISBN 1-85697-877-7

Printed in Great Britain

A · TREASURY · OF STORIES · FROM THE BROTHERS GRIMM

RETOLD BY
Jenny Koralek

ILLUSTRATED BY
Robin Lawrie

Kingfisher

NEW YORK

CONTENTS

HANSEL AND GRETEL

There was once a poor woodcutter who lived at the edge of a great forest with his two children, a boy named Hansel and a girl named Gretel. Their mother had died long ago and the woodcutter had married again, so they had a stepmother.

The family was already very poor indeed and often went hungry, and once, when there was a great famine in the land, the woodcutter could not provide even a crust of bread for them.

One evening, as he lay in bed tossing and turning with the worry of it, he sighed and said to his wife, "What will become of us? How can we feed the children, let alone ourselves?"

"I'll tell you what, husband," said his wife, "early tomorrow morning we will take them into the thickest part of the forest, light a fire, and give them each a little piece of bread. Then we will go to our work and leave them alone, so they will not find the way home again, and we shall be rid of them."

"No, wife," said the woodcutter, "that I can never do. I would not have the heart to leave my children all alone in the forest, for the wild animals would soon come and tear them to pieces."

"Oh, you fool!" said his wife. "Then all four of us will die of hunger. You might as well plane the wood for our coffins now." And she left him no peace till sadly he agreed to go along with her plan.

The two children, however, had also not been able to sleep for hunger, and so they overheard what their stepmother said. Gretel wept bitterly and said to Hansel, "What will become of us?"

"Be quiet, Gretel," said Hansel, "and don't cry—I will take care of you."

And as soon as their parents had fallen asleep, he got up, put on his coat, and, unlocking the back door, slipped out. The moon shone brightly, and the white pebbles that lay on the ground glittered so brightly that they looked like silver coins. Hansel bent down and put as many into his pocket as it would hold, and then he said to Gretel as he went back to bed, "It's all right, Gretel. Go to sleep now. God will help us."

The next morning before the sun rose, the stepmother woke the two children. "Get up, you lazy things," she said, "we are going into the forest to chop wood." Then she gave them each a piece of bread, saying, "Here is something for your dinner. Don't eat it before then, for you won't get anything else."

Gretel put the bread in her apron pocket, for Hansel's pocket was full of pebbles, and they all set out for the forest. When they had gone a little way Hansel stood still and stared back at the house. He did this several times, till his father said, "Hansel, what are you staring at, and why are you dawdling? Hurry up and look where you're going!"

"I was just looking at my white cat," said Hansel, "sitting on the roof of the house, trying to say good-bye."

"You silly boy!" said the stepmother. "That's not a cat; it's only the sun shining on the white chimney." But Hansel had not been looking at the cat; every time he stopped he had dropped one of the white pebbles out of his pocket onto the path.

When they came to the middle of the forest the woodcutter said, "Now children, collect some wood, and I will make you a fire, so that you will not be cold."

So Hansel and Gretel gathered together a big pile of twigs, and when the fire was lit, their stepmother said, "Now children, sit down near the fire and rest while we go into the forest and chop wood. When we've finished we'll come and fetch you."

Hansel and Gretel sat down by the fire and, when it was noon, ate the bread, and because they could hear the blows of an ax, they thought their father was near; but it was not an ax, but a branch that he had tied to a withered tree, which was being blown around by the wind. They waited so long and grew so tired that they fell fast asleep. When they woke up it was pitch dark, and Gretel began to cry, "How shall we ever get out of the forest?"

Hansel tried to comfort her by saying, "We have only to wait till the moon rises, and then we will quickly find the way."

The moon soon rose up brightly, and Hansel, taking his sister's hand, followed the pebbles, which glittered like new silver coins and showed them the path. All night long they walked on, and as day broke they came to their father's house. They knocked at the door, and when their stepmother opened it and saw Hansel and Gretel standing there she hid her fury by saying, "You naughty children! Why did you sleep so long in the forest? We thought you were never coming home again." But their father was very glad to see them, for it had broken his heart to leave them all alone.

Not long afterward there was once more a great famine in every corner of the land, and one night the children overheard their stepmother saying to their father, "There's no more to eat except this small loaf. That's it then, the children must be sent away. We will take them deeper into the forest, so that this time they will not find the way out. It is the only way to save us from starving to death."

The woodcutter was heartbroken and thought that he would rather share the last crust with the children. But his wife would not listen to a word he said and scolded and nagged him without end, until he gave in to her as he had before.

The children, however, were still awake and

overheard the conversation. As soon as their parents were asleep Hansel got up to collect some pebbles as he had before, but the stepmother had locked the door, so he could not get out. All the same he comforted Gretel, saying, "Don't cry! Go to sleep. God will help us."

Early in the morning the stepmother came and dragged them out of bed and gave them each a slice of bread even smaller than the time before. On the way to the forest Hansel crumbled his piece in his pocket, and every now and then dropped a crumb on the path.

"Hansel, why do you keep stopping and looking around?" said the woodcutter.

"I am looking at my little dove," answered Hansel, "nodding good-bye to me."

"Silly boy!" said the stepmother. "That's not a dove, but only the sun shining on the chimney." But Hansel still kept on dropping crumbs as he went along.

The stepmother led the children deep into the forest, where they had never been before, and when she had made them a huge fire she said to them, "Sit down here and rest, and if you feel tired have a little sleep. We're going into the forest to chop wood, and in the evening, when we've finished, we will come and fetch you."

When noon came Gretel shared her bread with Hansel, because he had scattered all of his on the path. Then they went to sleep, but in the evening no one came to fetch the poor children. It was pitch dark when they awoke, and Hansel comforted his sister by saying, "Just wait, Gretel, till the moon comes out, then we shall see the crumbs of bread that I have dropped, and they will show us the way home."

But when the moon rose and they got up, they could not see any crumbs, for the birds that had been flying around in the woods and fields had eaten them all up. Hansel kept saying, "It's all right, Gretel, we will soon find the way." But they did not, and they walked the whole night long and the next day, and they still had not found their way out but only got deeper and deeper into the forest. Hansel knew that if help did not come very soon they would die of hunger.

Suddenly they saw a beautiful snow-white bird sitting on the branch of a tree singing so sweetly that they stood still and listened to it. Then it stopped singing and flew off. The children followed it until it arrived at a cottage, where it perched on the roof. When Hansel and Gretel went close up to the cottage they saw that it was made of gingerbread and cakes, and the windowpanes of barley sugar.

"Let's go in there," said Hansel, "and have a glorious feast. I will eat a piece of the roof, and you can eat the window. Won't that be delicious?"

And he reached up and broke a piece off the roof in order to see how it tasted, while Gretel went up to the window and began to nibble at it.

Then a sweet voice called out from the room, "*Tip-tap, tip-tap*, who raps at my door?"

"The wind, the wind, only the wind," answered the children and they went on eating.

Hansel thought the roof tasted very nice, and so he tore off a great big piece, while Gretel broke a large round pane out of the window and sat down happily to eat it. Just then the door opened, and a very old woman came out leaning on a stick. Hansel and Gretel were so frightened that they dropped what they had in their hands, but the old woman just smiled and said, "Ah, you dear children, what has brought you here? Come in and stay with me, and you will come to no harm." Then she took them both by the hand and led them into her cottage.

First she sat them down to a good meal of milk and pancakes with sugar, apples, and nuts. Then she showed them two dear little beds covered with fresh white sheets. Hansel and Gretel lay down and thought they were in heaven.

Now the old woman was only pretending to be kind to the children: she was really a wicked witch who lay in wait for children and had built the

gingerbread house to tempt them in. Witches have red eyes and cannot see very far, but they have a fine sense of smell, so they know when children are nearby.

Early next morning before Hansel and Gretel woke up, she crept in to look at them lying there fast asleep with their rosy cheeks. "They will make a tasty meal or two!" she mumbled to herself. Then she dragged Hansel out of bed with her rough hand and shut him up in a little cage and slammed the door on him, and although he screamed loudly it was of no use.

Then the witch dragged poor Gretel out of bed, shaking her till she awoke, and said, "Get up, you lazy thing, and fetch some water to cook something good for your brother, who must stay in that cage and get fat, and when he is fat enough I shall eat him." Gretel began to cry, but it was no use: she had to do what the old witch wanted. So a nice meal was cooked for Hansel, but Gretel got only a crab's claw.

Every morning the old witch came to the cage and said, "Hansel, hold out your finger, so I can feel if you are getting fat." But Hansel would hold out a chicken bone, and the old witch, who had very bad sight, thought it was his finger and wondered very much why he was not getting any plumper.

When four weeks had gone by and Hansel was still quite thin, the witch lost all her patience. "I can't wait any longer," she said. "Gretel!" she called out in a rage. "Get some water quickly! Fat or lean, I'm going to kill Hansel this morning and eat him."

Oh, how poor Gretel grieved as she was forced to fetch the water, with tears pouring down her cheeks! "Dear, good God, help us now!" she cried. "If only we had been eaten by the wild animals in the forest, then at least we would have died together."

But the old witch called out, "It's no good crying like that: it won't help you one little bit."

So Gretel was forced to go and fill the biggest pot with water and make a fire. "First we will bake, however," said the old witch, "I have already heated the oven and kneaded the dough." And she pushed poor Gretel up to the oven, out of which the flames were burning fiercely.

"Get in," said the witch, "and see if it is hot enough, and then we will put in the bread," but she really meant to shut Gretel up in the oven and let her bake, so that she could eat her up as well as Hansel.

Gretel guessed what she was going to do and said, "I don't know how to get in."

"You silly goose," said the witch, "the opening is big enough. Look! I could even get in myself!" and she put her head into the oven.

Quickly Gretel gave the witch a big push, so that she fell right in, then she slammed the iron door shut and bolted it. Oh, how horribly the wicked witch howled! But Gretel ran away and left her to burn to ashes.

She ran to Hansel and, opening the cage door, called out, "Hansel, we are saved; the old witch is dead!" Out he sprang, like a bird out of his cage when the door is opened, and the two children hugged and kissed each other over and over again.

And now, as there was nothing to fear, they went into the witch's house, where in every corner were caskets full of pearls and other precious jewels. "These are better than pebbles," said Hansel, putting as many into his pocket as it would hold while Gretel filled her apron.

"And now let's get out of this enchanted forest."

When they had walked for two hours they came to a large stretch of water.

"How will we get over?" said Hansel. "There's no bridge."

"And no boat either," said Gretel, "but there swims a white duck. I will ask her to help us over." And she sang,

> "Little duck, good little duck,
> Gretel and Hansel, here we stand.
> There is neither boat nor bridge;
> Take us on your back to land."

So the duck came to them, and Hansel climbed on and told his sister sit behind him.

"No," said Gretel, "that will be too much for the duck; we'd better cross over one at a time."

When the good little bird had carried them both to the other side they soon came to a forest, which they knew better and better at every step, and at last they saw their father's house. Then they began to run and, bursting into the house, they flung themselves into his arms. He had not had one happy hour since he had left the children in the forest, and the cruel stepmother was dead. Gretel shook her apron, and the pearls and other precious jewels rolled out upon the floor, and Hansel threw down one handful after the other out of his pocket. Then all their sorrows were ended, and they lived together in great happiness.

My tale is done. There runs a mouse; whoever catches her may make a great, great cap out of her fur.

THE MUSICIANS OF BREMEN

There was once a donkey who had been a faithful servant to a farmer for many years, but was now growing old and every day more and more unfit for work. The farmer was tired of keeping him and began to think about killing him off. But the donkey guessed what the farmer had in mind and when no one was looking, he nudged the stable door open and trotted away toward the great city of Bremen. After all, he said to himself, I bray so beautifully, in Bremen I could easily become a musician.

After he had traveled a little way, he spotted a dog lying by the roadside panting as if he was very tired.

"What makes you pant so, my friend?" asked the donkey.

"Oh!" howled the dog. "My master was going

to kill me, because I am old and weak and can no longer go hunting with him, so I ran away. But what can I do to earn my living?"

"Well, listen to me!" said the donkey. "I am going to the great city of Bremen to become a musician. Why don't you come with me and see if you can become a musician too?"

The dog decided to go with the donkey so they trotted on together, but had not gone far before they saw a cat sitting in the middle of the road looking extremely scared and very miserable.

"Good day, cat!" said the donkey. "What's the matter with you? You look quite wretched."

"Oh!" meowed the cat. "How could I be anything else when my life is in danger? Because I am getting old and would rather lie by the fire than run about chasing after mice, my mistress grabbed hold of me and was going to drown me. Luckily I got away from her, but I don't know how I am going to earn my living."

"Well," said the donkey, "why don't you come with us to the great city of Bremen: you are a good night singer and will surely make a fortune as a musician."

The cat liked this idea very much, and so she happily joined the company.

Soon afterward, as they were passing by a farmyard, they saw a rooster perched on a gate, crowing his head off.

"Bravo!" said the donkey. "You're making a fine noise I must say. What's it all about?"

"Well!" said the rooster. "I was telling everyone we are having fine weather today, but the farmer's wife doesn't want to know and is threatening to cut off my head tomorrow and cook me for the guests who are coming to dinner on Sunday!"

"We can't let that happen!" said the donkey. "Come with us, Mister Chanticleer; it will be better than staying here to have your head cut off! Besides, who knows? If we learn to sing in tune together, we could perform some kind of concert: so why don't you come along with us?"

"What an excellent idea," said the rooster, so the four of them went merrily on their way.

But by nightfall they had still not reached the great city of Bremen, so they went into a forest to sleep. The donkey and the dog lay down under a great tree, and the cat climbed up into the branches. Meanwhile the rooster, thinking that the higher he sat the safer he would be, flew up to the very top of the tree. While he was looking around to make sure everything was all right, as he always did before he went to sleep, he saw something bright and shining in the distance. He called down to his companions and said, "There must be a house over there: I can see a light."

"If that's so," said the donkey, "let's go and have a look. It's not that comfortable out here."

"Besides," added the dog, "I wouldn't say no to a bone or two, or a bit of meat."

So they set off toward the spot where Chanticleer had seen the light, till they came to a house where a gang of robbers lived.

The donkey, being the tallest of the company, marched straight up to the window and peeked in.

"Well, donkey," said Chanticleer, "what can you see?"

"What can I see?" replied the donkey. "Why, I see a table laden with all kinds of delicious food and drink, and robbers sitting around it stuffing themselves and making merry."

"That would be just the house for us," said the rooster.

"Yes," said the donkey, "if we could only get in." After a long whispered discussion about how to get the robbers out of the house, they at last hit upon a plan. The donkey stood upright on his hindlegs, with his forefeet resting on the windowsill; the dog climbed onto his back; the cat scrambled onto the dog's shoulders; and the rooster flew up and sat on the cat's head; and then they began their music.

The donkey brayed, the dog barked, the cat meowed, and the rooster crowed. Then they crashed through the window and tumbled into the room in a shower of broken glass, which made a hideous crash.

The robbers, who had been very frightened by the opening concert, now believed that some frightful hobgoblin had broken in, and they ran away as fast as their legs would carry them.

Our musicians quickly sat down and finished off the food as if they did not expect to eat again for a month. When they were well and truly full, they put out the lights, and each chose a resting place to his or her own liking. The donkey lay down on a heap of straw in the yard; the dog stretched himself out on a mat behind the door; the cat curled herself up in front of the fire; and the rooster perched on the roof of the house. They were all rather tired by now and soon fell asleep.

But when the robbers saw from a safe distance that the lights were out and that all seemed quiet, they began to wonder if they had been in too great a hurry to run away; and one of them, who was braver than the rest, went to see what was going on. Finding everything quiet he marched into the kitchen and groped about for a match in order to light a candle. Then he saw the glittering fiery eyes of the cat, and mistaking them for live coals, stuck the match into them to light it. But the cat did not find this at all funny and leaped at his face, spitting and scratching. This frightened him so much that he ran to the back door, but there the dog jumped up and bit him in the leg, and as he was crossing over the yard the donkey kicked him, and the

rooster, who had been awakened by the noise, crowed with all his might.

At this the robber ran back as fast as he could to his comrades and told the captain how a horrid witch had got into the house and had spat at him and scratched his face with her long, bony fingers, how a man with a knife in his hand had hidden himself behind the door and stabbed him in the leg, how a monster stood in the yard and struck him with a club, and how the devil sat on the roof crying, "Throw the rascal up here!"

After this the robbers never dared to go back to the house; but the musicians were so pleased with their new home that they stayed there and, as far as I know, they are still there to this very day.

THE WATER OF LIFE

Once upon a time there was a king who was so ill that everybody feared he was going to die. His three sons were very sad and went out into the palace gardens to cry. There they met an old man, who asked them why they were crying. The princes told him their father was so ill that he was sure to die, for nothing could save him.

The old man said, "I know a way to save him: a drink from the water of life will make him better, but it is very difficult to find."

"I will soon find it," said the eldest son, and he went to the sick king and begged him to let him set out at once in search of the water of life, which alone could save him.

"No," said the king, "the danger is too great. I would rather die."

But the son begged and begged until at last the king consented. The prince went on his way, thinking in his heart that if he brought the water he would be the dearest to his father and would inherit his kingdom.

After he had ridden a long way he met a dwarf on the road.

"Where are you off to in such a hurry?" asked the dwarf.

"That's none of your business, you ugly little man," said the prince rudely, and he rode off. But the dwarf was angry and made an evil wish, so that soon after, the prince came into a narrow mountain pass and the farther he rode the narrower it grew, till at last it was so narrow that he could not go on, but he could not turn his horse around either, or dismount, and he sat there, helplessly trapped.

Meanwhile the sick king waited and waited for him, but he did not come, so the second son asked his father to let him go too and seek the water of life. If my brother is dead the kingdom comes to me, he thought to himself.

At first the king refused to let him go, but in the end he gave in, and the prince set out on the same road as the elder one had taken and met the same dwarf, who stopped him and asked him, "Where are you off to in such a hurry?"

"Mind your own business, you ugly little man,"

said the prince, and he rode off without looking back. But the dwarf put a spell on him, and the same thing happened to him as it had to his brother: he came to a place that was so narrow that he could move neither forward nor backward. That's what happens to haughty people.

Now, when the second son did not return, the youngest prince begged to be allowed to go and fetch the water of life, and in the end the king gave his consent.

The youngest son also met the dwarf and was asked where he was going in such a hurry. The youngest son stopped and said, "I am seeking the water of life for my father who is dying."

"Do you know where to find it?" asked the dwarf.

"No," replied the prince.

"Since you are so gentle and polite," said the dwarf, "and not haughty and rude like your dishonest brothers, I will help you and tell you where you can find the water of life. It flows from a fountain in the court of an enchanted castle, which you will never get into unless I give you an iron rod and two loaves of bread. With the rod knock three times at the iron door of the castle, and it will spring open. Two lions will be lying there with open jaws, but if you throw them each a loaf of bread they will be quiet. Then hurry to the fountain and fetch some of the water of life before the clock strikes twelve, for then the door will shut again, and you will be imprisoned forever."

The prince thanked the dwarf and, taking the rod and the bread, he set out on his journey. When he arrived at the castle he found everything just as the dwarf had said. At the third knock the door sprang open, and when the prince had quietened the two snarling lions with the bread, he walked into a large and splendid hall. There he saw a sword and some bread lying on the ground, which he picked up and took with him. A little farther on he came to a room where a beautiful maiden was standing. She threw her arms around the startled prince and explained that he had freed her from an evil spell. She told the prince that if he came back in a year she would marry him and give him her whole kingdom. Then she told him where the fountain of the water of life was, and he hurried away before the clock struck twelve. But next he came to a room with a fine clean bed, and being tired he lay down to rest for a moment. But as soon as his head hit the pillow he fell fast asleep.

When he woke up the clock was striking a quarter to twelve, and the sound made him hurry to the fountain and quickly pour some water into a cup standing there. Then he ran to the door, and only just got out before the clock struck twelve. The door swung to so heavily that it scraped off the skin of his heel.

But he was thrilled, in spite of this, that he had now got some of the water of life for his father. On his way home he met the dwarf again, and when the dwarf saw the sword and bread that he had brought away he said he had done well, for with the sword he could destroy whole armies, and the bread would never come to an end.

Now the prince was not willing to return home to his father without his brothers, and so he said to the dwarf, "Dear dwarf, can you tell me where my brothers are? They went out before me in search of the water of life but never returned."

"They are stuck fast between two mountains," replied the dwarf. "I put a spell on them because they were so rude and haughty."

The prince begged for his brothers' freedom, and finally the dwarf agreed to let them go, but he warned the youngest son to beware of them, for they had evil in their hearts.

The prince was overjoyed to see his brothers and told them everything that had happened to him. How he had found the water of life and

brought away a cupful of it; and how he had
rescued a beautiful princess, who was going to wait
for him for a whole year, and then he was to return
and marry her and be given a rich kingdom.

After this tale the three brothers rode away
together, and soon came to a land where war and
famine were raging. The youngest prince went to
the king of this land and gave him the bread, with
which all the people were fed. The prince then
gave him the sword and the king killed all his
enemies, so that there was peace again. Then the
prince took back the bread and sword and rode on
with his brothers, and they came to two other
countries where war and famine were destroying
the people. The prince lent his bread and sword to
two more kings, and so saved three kingdoms
altogether. Then they came to a ship and set sail
over the sea for home.

During the voyage the two elder brothers said to each other, "Our brother has found the water of life and we have not, so our father will give the kingdom that belongs to us to him and we will have nothing. We can't let that happen." They became so jealous of their brother that one day when he was fast asleep, they poured the water of life out of his cup into a bottle of their own and filled his cup with bitter salt water. As soon as they arrived home the youngest brother took his cup to his dying father, but the king had only taken a few sips of the water when he grew more ill than ever, for it was as bitter as wormwood.

Then the two elder princes, who had been spying through the keyhole, burst into the room and accused their brother of poisoning their father. "We are the ones who have brought you the water of life," they said and they handed their cup to the king. Before he had drunk half the water the king felt his sickness leave him, and soon he was as strong and healthy as in his young days.

The two brothers went to see the youngest prince in his chamber, and they sneered at him, saying, "You certainly found the water of life, but you had the trouble and we had the reward. You should have been more careful and kept your eyes open, for we took your cup and changed the water while you were asleep and, what's more, in a year one of us will go and marry your princess. It's no good telling the king. He will not believe you, and if you say a single word we will kill you, but if you keep your mouth shut you will be safe."

The old king was very angry with his youngest son, because he believed he had tried to kill him. He decided that the prince should be secretly shot, and a huntsman was sent with him when he went riding in the forest to do the evil deed. But when they were alone in the forest, the huntsman seemed so sad that the prince asked him what was the matter with him.

"I cannot tell you and yet I must tell you," said the huntsman.

"Be brave and tell me what it is," said the prince, "and I will forgive you."

"Oh!" sighed the huntsman. "The king has ordered me to shoot you."

The prince was frightened and said, "Don't kill me, dear huntsman, don't kill me! I will give you

my royal coat and you shall give me yours in exchange."

The huntsman happily agreed to this, for he had no wish to shoot the prince, and after they had exchanged clothes the huntsman went home, while the prince went deeper into the forest.

A few days later three wagons laden with gold and precious stones arrived at the king's palace for his youngest son. They were gifts from the three kings in gratitude for the sword that had killed their enemies and the bread that had fed their starving people. When he saw these gifts the old king said, "Perhaps, after all, my son was innocent," and he wept and wished he had not let his son be killed.

The huntsman heard what the king was saying and cried out, "He is not dead! For I could not find it in my heart to obey you," and he told the king what had happened. The king felt as if a stone had been removed from his heart, and he sent out messages throughout his kingdom that his son could come home and once more know his father's love.

Meanwhile the princess had ordered a road of

pure shining gold to be made right up to her castle. She told her servants that whoever came riding straight up this road was the right person and should be allowed into the castle, but, whoever rode up by the side road was not to be allowed in because he was not the right person.

So when the year was up the eldest brother thought he would hurry to the castle and take the princess as his bride and the kingdom besides. So he rode away, and when he came to the castle and saw the fine golden road he thought it would be a shame to spoil such valuable gold by riding on it, so he turned to the left and rode up the side road.

But when he came to the door the guards told him he was not the right person, and he must ride away again. Soon afterward the second prince also set out, and he too, when he came to the golden road and his horse set its forefeet upon it, thought it would be a pity to ride on it. So he turned to the right and went up the side road, and when he came to the gate the guards refused to let him in and told him he was not the person expected, so he had to go home too.

The youngest prince, who had all this time been wandering around in the forest, had also remembered that the year was up. Soon after his brothers had left he arrived at the castle and rode straight up the golden road, for he was so busy thinking about his beloved princess that he did not even notice it! As soon as he arrived at the door it was opened, and the princess kissed him joyfully.

They got married the very next day and then
the princess told her husband that his father had
forgiven him and longed to see him. So they rode
to the old king's palace, and the prince told his
father what his brothers had done while he slept,
and how they had sworn him to silence. When the
king heard this he was furious and wanted to
punish his wicked sons, but they had very wisely
taken themselves off in a ship and never dared
come home again.

SNOW-WHITE AND ROSE-RED

There was once a poor widow who lived in a cottage with her two daughters, who were named Snow-White and Rose-Red, because they were as lovely as the flowers that grew on two rosebushes outside the cottage door. They were both happy, hardworking, and friendly children. Snow-White was quieter and more gentle than Rose-Red, who loved to run around in the meadows, picking flowers or chasing butterflies, while Snow-White stayed at home helping their mother with the housework or reading to her if there was nothing else to do.

The two children loved each other dearly and went everywhere hand-in-hand. They had long ago agreed that they would never be parted from each other and would always share everything. They often went deep into the forest to pick wild berries, but no animal ever harmed them: the hare would eat out of their hands, the deer did not run away from them, and the birds went on singing as if nobody were there.

Snow-White and Rose-Red kept their mother's cottage so clean that it was a pleasure to enter it. Every morning in the summertime Rose-Red would pick her mother a white rosebud and a red rosebud, and every winter's morning Snow-White would light the fire and put the kettle on to boil, and although the kettle was made of copper, it shone like gold, because she polished it so well.

In the evenings, when snowflakes were falling, the mother would say, "Snow-White, go and bolt the door." And when they were all sitting by the fire the mother would put on her spectacles and read wonderful stories to Snow-White and Rose-Red out of a big book, while close by their side lay a little lamb, and on a perch behind them a little white dove slept with her head under her wing.

One evening, when they were sitting comfortably together, there was a knock at the door. "Hurry, Rose-Red!" cried her mother. "Go and open the door; perhaps it's a traveler who needs shelter."

So Rose-Red went and drew back the bolt and opened the door, expecting to see some poor man outside. But there, towering above her, was a huge

black bear. Rose-Red screamed and jumped back. The little lamb bleated, the dove fluttered on her perch, and Snow-White hid behind her mother's bed.

The bear, however, began to speak, and said gently, "Don't be afraid, I won't hurt you; but I am half-frozen and would like to come in and warm myself."

"Poor bear!" cried the mother. "Come in and lie down by the fire; but be careful not to singe your fur." Then she said, "Come here, Rose-Red and Snow-White, the bear won't hurt you, he is quite friendly." So they both came back, and little by little the lamb and the dove also stopped being afraid of this unexpected visitor.

"Now, dear children!" said the bear. "Before I come in please brush the snow off my coat." So they fetched their brooms and brushed him down. Then he stretched himself out in front of the fire and growled happily, and before long the children lost their fear enough to play games with the clumsy animal. They tugged at his long, shaggy coat, rested their little feet on his back, and rolled him over backward and forward, laughing when he growled at them.

The bear put up with all their tricks patiently, and when the children had gone to bed, their mother said to the bear, "You may sleep here by the fire if you like, safe from the cold weather."

Next morning the two children let the bear out

again, and he trotted away over the snow, and all through the winter he came back every evening at the same time. He would lie down by the fire and let the children play with him as much as they liked, until in the end they got so used to him that the door was always left unbolted for him.

But when the spring came, and everything out of doors was green again, the bear told Snow-White that he must go away for the whole summer.

"Where are you going, then, dear bear?" asked Snow-White.

"I must go into the forest and guard my treasures from the evil dwarfs," said the bear, "for in winter, when the earth is frozen, they have to stay down in their holes and cannot work their way through the hard ground. But now the sun has thawed the earth and warmed it, the dwarfs break through and steal anything they can find, and once they get their hands on something and hide it in their caves, it is not easily found again."

Snow-White was very sad that the bear was leaving and opened the door so unwillingly that as he squeezed through it a piece of his hairy coat got caught on the latch. Through the small tear in his coat Snow-White thought she saw the glittering of gold, but she was not quite sure if she had imagined it, and before she could take a closer look, the bear ran quickly away and was soon out of sight behind the trees.

Not long afterward the mother sent the children into the forest to collect firewood. They came to a tree that was lying across the path, and near the trunk something was bobbing up and down. Snow-White and Rose-Red could not imagine what it was, but when they got closer they saw a dwarf with an old wrinkled face and a very long white beard. The end of this beard was stuck fast in a crack of the tree, and the little man kept jumping around like a dog tied to a chain, because he did not know how to free himself.

He glared at the two girls with his red, fiery eyes and yelled, "Well, don't just stand there. Surely you are not going to walk past without offering me any help?"

"What happened?" asked Rose-Red.

"You stupid, gawping goose!" screeched the dwarf. "I was trying to split the tree to get a little wood for my kitchen fire. I had driven the wedge in correctly, and everything was going well, when suddenly the wedge fell out and the split in the tree closed up so quickly that I did not have time to pull my beautiful beard out, and now I'm stuck! Don't laugh at me, you horrid girls! Do something!"

The children did everything they could to pull the dwarf's beard out, but without success until Snow-White remembered the scissors in her pocket. She took them out and cut off the end of his beard.

As soon as the dwarf was free he snatched up his gold-filled sack, which had been lying between the roots of the tree, and, throwing it over his shoulder, he marched off, grumbling and groaning and crying, "Stupid girl! Fancy cutting off a piece of my beautiful beard. I wish you nothing but bad luck!" And away he went.

A few days later Snow-White and Rose-Red went fishing, and as they came to the pond they saw something like a great locust hopping around on the bank. It seemed to be in danger of falling into the water. They ran up and saw it was the dwarf.

"Whatever are you doing?" asked Rose-Red. "If you're not careful you will fall in."

"Oh, you silly girl!" snarled the dwarf. "Can't you see this fish is trying to pull me in? My beard has got tangled up in my fishing line. Do something quickly, can't you?"

So once again Snow-White pulled out her scissors and cut off another piece of his beard.

When the dwarf saw what she had done he was furious and yelled, "You foolish thing! Do you want me to be ugly? It was bad enough that you had to cut it once, but now I won't dare show myself to the other dwarfs. I wish I had never set eyes on either of you!" Then he picked up a bag of pearls lying in the rushes and, without another word, slipped off and disappeared behind a stone.

Not many days after this adventure the mother sent the two girls to town to buy needles and thread and some laces and ribbons. They were walking along when suddenly they saw a great bird circling overhead. Every now and then it would swoop lower and lower, till at last it flew down behind a rock. They heard a piercing shriek and, running up, they saw with horror that the eagle had caught the same old dwarf and was trying to carry him off. The kind children grabbed hold of his feet and hung on to him till the bird let go and flew off.

As soon as the dwarf had recovered from his fright, he yelled at them, "Couldn't you have held me more gently? You have torn my fine brown coat, you clumsy, meddling fools!" Then he picked up a bag filled with precious stones and vanished among the rocks.

Snow-White and Rose-Red walked on to the town and did their shopping. They were on their way home when they stumbled on the dwarf yet again. He was shaking out his bag of precious stones thinking nobody was near. The bright jewels glittered in the sunshine as beautifully as a rainbow, and the two girls stopped to admire the heap of rubies, emeralds, and sapphires.

"What are you staring at?" snapped the dwarf, his face growing as red as copper with rage. He started shouting and screaming at the poor girls, when all of a sudden there was a loud roaring noise and a great black bear came lumbering out of the forest. The dwarf was terrified and tried to run away but the bear soon had him between his paws.

"Spare me, my dear Lord Bear!" screeched the dwarf. "I will give you all my treasures. Look at these beautiful jewels! Don't kill me! What have you to fear from a weakling like me? Look at those two wicked girls! Eat them! They would make a tasty meal—they're as fat as butter. Eat them, for heaven's sake!"

But the bear, without a word, gave the ungrateful,

thieving dwarf a single blow with one huge paw, and that was the end of him.

The girls were about to run away, when the bear called after them, "Snow-White and Rose-Red, don't be frightened! Wait, for I will come with you." Then they recognized his voice and stopped. As the bear came toward  them, his rough black coat suddenly fell off, and there stood a tall man dressed entirely in gold.

Snow-White and Rose-Red could not believe their eyes.

"I am a king's son," he said. "The wicked dwarf turned me into a bear and then stole all my treasures. Only his death could break the spell. Now he has received his well-deserved punishment, and I am a prince again."

Then they all went home, and Snow-White was married to the prince, and Rose-Red to his brother. They shared the immense treasure among them all, and the old mother lived for many years happily with her two children and their husbands.

The rosebushes that had stood outside the cottage door were planted at the palace gate where their red and white flowers grew more and more beautiful every year.

THE WOLF AND THE SEVEN LITTLE KIDS

Once upon a time there was an old goat who had seven kids whom she loved as every mother loves her children.

One day she wanted to go into the forest to fetch some food, so she called the seven kids together and said, "Dear children, I am going away into the forest. Be on your guard against the wolf, for if he comes here he will eat you up—skin, hair, and all. He often disguises himself, but you will know him by his rough voice and his black feet."

The little kids said, "Don't worry, dear mother, we will be very careful while you are away." So the old goat bleated good-bye and went off with a quiet mind.

Not long afterward, somebody knocked at the door and called out, "Open the door, dear children!

It's your mother and I've brought you each a present."

But the little kids knew from the rough voice that it was the wolf, and so they said, "We will not open the door—you're not our mother. She has a soft and loving voice, but yours is gruff. You are a wolf!"

So the wolf went to a shop and bought a big piece of chalk, which he ate to make his voice softer. Then he came back, knocked at the door and called out, "Open the door, dear children; your mother has come home and has brought you each a present."

But the wolf had put his black paws on the windowsill, so the kids saw them and said, "No, we will not open the door. Our mother hasn't got black feet. You are a wolf!"

So the wolf went to the baker and said, "I have hurt my foot, put some dough on it." And when the baker had done so, he ran to the miller and said, "Sprinkle some white flour on my feet." But the miller, thinking he was up to some mischief, hesitated until the wolf said, "If you don't do it at once, I will gobble you up." This frightened the miller into sprinkling the wolf's feet with flour.

Then the wicked wolf went to the goat's hut for the third time and, knocking at the door, called out, "Open to me, my children; it's your own dear mother, and I've brought something for each of you out of the forest."

"First show us your feet," said the kids, "so that we may see if you really are our mother." So the wolf put his feet up on the windowsill, and when the kids saw that they were white, they thought it was their mother and opened the door. Then who should come in but the wolf! The kids were terrified and tried to hide themselves. One ran under the table, the second got into the bed, the third into the cupboard, the fourth into an empty bucket, the fifth into the oven, and the sixth into the washtub. But the wolf found them all and swallowed them all up one after the other. The only one he did not find was the seventh and youngest kid who was hiding in the grandfather clock.

When the wolf was full up he dragged himself out into the green meadow where he lay down under a tree and fell fast asleep.

What a sight the old goat saw when she came home from the forest! The door stood wide open; the table, chairs, and buckets were overturned; the washtub was broken to pieces; and the sheets and pillows pulled off the bed. She searched high and low for her children but could not find them anywhere. She called them by name, one after the other; but no one answered. At last, when she came to the name of the youngest, a little voice replied, "Here I am, dear mother, in the grandfather clock." The old goat took her out and heard how the wolf had come and gobbled up all the others. You can have

no idea how long she wept for her poor little ones.

At last, still weeping, she went outside with the young kid running along behind her; and when they came to the meadow, there lay the wolf under the tree, snoring so heavily that the earth itself shook. The old goat walked all around him, and saw that something was moving around in the wolf's belly.

"Goodness me!" she cried. "Is it possible that my poor children are still alive?!" And she quickly ran home and fetched a pair of scissors and a needle and thread. Then she cut open the wicked wolf's hairy belly and had hardly made the first slit when one little kid put his head out, and as she cut further, out jumped all six, one after the other, still alive and unhurt, for the greedy wolf in his eager haste had gulped them down all in one piece.

And then what joy there was! The seven little kids hugged their mother and jumped about like dancing fleas.

But their mother said, "Hurry up, go and find some large stones, so we can fill up the wolf's belly while he is still asleep." So the seven kids quickly collected up a pile of stones and put them in the wolf's belly until there was no more room. Then their mother crept up and took a good look at the wolf to make sure he was still fast asleep and then she sewed up the slit.

When the wolf at last woke up, he got heavily to his feet and, because the stones lying in his belly made him feel thirsty, he went in search of a stream to have a good long drink of water. But as he

staggered along
the stones began
to tumble around in
his belly, and he called
out;

> "What rattles, what rattles
> Against my poor bones?
> Not little goats, I think,
> But only big stones!"

When the wolf came to the stream and stooped down to drink, the heavy stones made him lose his balance, so that he fell in and sank down, down, down into the water.

As soon as the seven kids saw this, they came running up, singing out loud, "The wolf is dead! Hurrah! Hurrah! The wolf is dead, hurrah!" and no wolf was ever able to play tricks on those seven kids again.

THE NOSE

Did you ever hear the story of the three poor soldiers on their way home from the wars, who begged as they went along?

They had journeyed a long way, when one evening they came to a deep, dark forest. There was no way around it, night was falling, and they had no choice but to sleep there.

They agreed to take turns keeping watch in case any wild animals should creep up on them and tear them to pieces.

The two who were to rest first lay down and fell fast asleep, and the other made himself a good fire under the trees and sat down to keep watch. He had not been sitting there long before all of a sudden a little man in a red jacket appeared.

"Who's there?" said the little man.

"A friend," said the soldier.

"What sort of a friend?"

"A penniless old soldier," said the other, "with his two comrades who have nothing left to live on, but come, sit down and warm yourself."

"Thank you kindly," said the little man, "and now let me do something for you; take this and show it to your comrades in the morning." And he took out an old cloak and gave it to the soldier.

"Whenever you put this over your shoulders," he said, "whatever you wish for will come true." Then the little man made him a bow and vanished into the forest.

The second soldier's turn to watch soon came. He had not been sitting by himself long when up came the little man in the red jacket again. The soldier treated him in just as friendly a way as his comrade had done, and the little man gave him a purse, which he told him was always full of gold, however much he took out of it.

Then the third soldier's turn to watch came, and once again the little man appeared and was invited to sit by the fire.

"You have been very kind to me," said the little

man, and he drew out a horn and said, "This is my gift to you. Whenever it is played crowds will gather, everyone will forget their troubles and dance to its beautiful music." And then he vanished.

In the morning each soldier told his story and showed his treasure, and since they all liked each other very much and were old friends, they agreed to travel together to see the world, and for a while only to make use of the wonderful purse. And they spent their time very joyfully until at last they grew tired of this roving life and decided to settle down.

So the first soldier put the cloak on and wished for a fine castle. In a flash it stood before their eyes with gardens and green lawns spread around it, and at that very moment a grand coach with three dapple-gray horses came out of the gate to meet them and bring them home.

It was not long before they grew tired of always staying at home, so they dressed up in their richest clothes and ordered their servants to bring out their coach with three horses, and they set out on a journey to visit a neighboring king. Now this king had an only daughter, and because he thought the three soldiers were princes, he gave them a kind welcome.

One day, as the second soldier was walking with the princess, she saw the magic purse in his hand. She asked him what it was, and he was foolish enough to tell her. Now this princess was secretly a very cunning and clever witch, so she set to work and made a purse exactly like the soldier's. Then she asked him to come and see her, and gave him so much wine to drink that he fell fast asleep. Then she took the magic purse out of his pocket and left the one she had made in its place.

The next morning the soldiers set out for home, and when they reached their castle they took out their purse to get some money and found to their great sorrow that when they had emptied it, no more money came in place of what they took. The second soldier guessed at once that the princess had tricked him.

"Alas!" he cried. "Whatever shall we do without any money?"

"Don't worry!" said the first soldier, "I will soon get the purse back."

Then he threw his cloak over his shoulders and said, "I wish to be in the princess's room." There he found her sitting alone counting out all the gold that was falling around her in a shower from the purse.

She looked up and saw the soldier and she started yelling, "Help! Help! Thieves! Thieves!" so loudly that the whole court came running.

The poor soldier was so terrified that he forgot his cloak was magic, ran to the open window, and jumped out. Unluckily in his haste his cloak got caught on a rosebush and was left hanging there, to the great joy of the princess, because she knew it was a magic cloak.

The poor soldier walked sadly back to the castle, but the third soldier said, "Cheer up! All is not lost!" and took out his horn and blew a merry tune. At the first blast a huge army of soldiers on horseback came rushing to help them. They surrounded the king's palace and told the king that he must give back the purse and cloak at once, or his kingdom would be utterly destroyed.

The king hurried to his daughter's room and told her what the soldiers were threatening.

"Just leave everything to me," she said confidently, "I will get rid of the lot of them."

Then she dressed up in rags like a poor girl and crept out at nightfall with her maid, and went into the enemy's camp with a basket full of trinkets on her arm.

In the morning she wandered about the camp singing so beautifully that all the soldiers rushed out of their tents and ran around this way and that, trying to catch a glimpse of her by following the sound of her voice.

Among them was the third soldier, who had forgotten all about his horn lying in his tent. It was easy enough in the commotion for the princess's maid to creep in and steal it.

Now the princess had all three magic gifts in her hands.

She and her maid slipped away to the palace, the army vanished into thin air, and the three soldiers were once again as penniless and forlorn as when the little man with the red jacket found them in the forest.

"Comrades," said the second soldier, who had had the purse, "we had better go our separate ways, and each seek our bread as best we can."

But the other two said they would rather stay together, so he set off by himself. After a while he came to a forest (which he did not know was the same forest where they had met with so much good luck before). He walked on till evening, when he sat down tired beneath a tree and soon fell asleep.

When he opened his eyes the next morning, he saw that the tree was laden with the most beautiful apples. He was by now very hungry, so he quickly picked and ate first one, then a second, then a third apple. A strange feeling came over his nose and when he put the fourth apple into his mouth something was in the way. He touched it and realized to his horror that it was his nose, which was growing and growing. He could see it had reached his chest. But it did not stop there: it grew on and on.

"Heavens!" he exclaimed. "Whenever will it stop growing!"

And well might he ask, for by this time it had reached the ground where he was sitting on the grass and kept getting heavier and heavier so he

could not stand up; and it seemed as if it would never end, for already it stretched its enormous length right through the forest.

Meanwhile his comrades were journeying on, till all of a sudden one of them tripped over something.

"What can that be?" said the other.

They looked and looked, and decided that the only thing it looked like was a nose.

"Let's follow it and see who it belongs to," they said. So they followed it and followed it, till at last they came to their poor comrade lying stretched out beneath the apple tree, all of a heap under the weight of the nose. They didn't know what to do. They tried to carry him, but in vain. So they sat down in despair, when suddenly the little man in the red jacket appeared out of nowhere.

"Well, my dear old friend!" he said, laughing when he saw that long, long nose. "I must find a cure for you."

"Pick a pear from that tree over there," he said. "Take one good bite and see what happens!"

The soldier did as he was told and at once his nose went back to its right size. He was overjoyed and thanked the little man with all his heart.

"That's not all!" said the little man. "I will do something else for you. Go to the princess and get her to eat some of your apples. Her nose will grow twenty times as long as yours did. Then look sharp, and you will get what you want of her."

They thanked their old friend very heartily for all his kindness and decided that the poor soldier who had already tried the power of the apple should dress up as a gardener's boy and go to the king's palace and say he had apples to sell, such as were never seen there before.

Off he went, and everyone who saw the apples wanted to taste them at once, but the soldier said they were only for the princess. As soon as she heard about the apples the princess sent her maid to buy every single one of them. They were so ripe and rosy that she began to gobble them up and had already eaten three when she began to wonder what was happening to her nose, which felt very strange. It began to grow, and then grew and grew down to the ground, out of the window, over the garden wall, and out of sight, and then who knows where?

The king offered a rich reward to whoever could heal her of this dreadful disease. Many tried, but the princess's nose did not get any shorter.

The three soldiers waited until the princess was desperate. Then the second soldier dressed himself up as a doctor and said he could cure her. He chopped up one of the magic apples, and to punish her a little more gave her just a few pieces saying he would call the next day to see how she was.

Of course, the next day, instead of being better, the nose had been growing fast all night, and the poor princess was in a terrible state. So the "doctor" chopped up a few tiny pieces of the magic pear, told her to eat it, and said he was sure that would help and that he would call again the next day. Sure enough next day the nose was a little smaller, but it was still bigger than it was before the so-called doctor had first began to meddle with it.

"I must frighten this cunning princess just a little bit more before I get what I want of her," said the second soldier, so he gave her another dose of the apple, and when he came back the next day the nose was ten times as bad as before.

"Your Highness," said the "doctor." "Something powerful is stopping my medicine from working and I know what it is; you have stolen some precious things. I know this for a fact, and if you do not give them back, I cannot cure you."

"I have certainly not stolen anything at all ever in my life!" said the princess.

"Very well," said the "doctor," "if you say so, but I know I am right, and you will die if you do not own up to it."

He went to the king and told him the whole story. The king was furious and ordered the wicked princess to give back the cloak, the purse, and the horn at once.

Then, and only then, did the princess tell her maid to fetch all three, and she gave them to the "doctor," and begged him to give them back to the soldiers. As soon as he had them safe he gave her a whole pear to eat, and immediately her nose went back to its right size.

Then, to the astonishment and fury of the princess, the "doctor" put on the cloak, wished the king and all his court a good day, and was soon back with his two comrades.

And from that time the three soldiers lived happily at home in their castle, except when they rode out in their coach drawn by the three dapple-gray horses.

OLD MOTHER FROST

There was once a widow who had two daughters, one of whom was beautiful and hardworking, and the other ugly and lazy. The widow was always kind, however, to the ugly one, because she was her own daughter; she made the other, who was her stepdaughter, do all the dirty work. The poor girl also had to sit by the well every day and do so much spinning that it made her fingers bleed.

One day the spindle was covered with so much blood that she knelt down by the well and tried to wash it, but it fell out of her hands into the water and sank to the bottom of the well.

She ran crying to her stepmother and told her what had happened. Her stepmother was very angry and said, "What am I supposed to do? *You* dropped it, so *you* must fetch it out again!" So the poor girl went back to the well, not knowing what to do, and in despair, jumped into the well to fetch the spindle out. As she fell she fainted, and when she came to she found herself in a beautiful sunny meadow, full of flowers. She got up and walked along till she came to an oven full of bread.

"Take us out! Take us out!" cried the loaves, "or we shall be burned. We have been baked long enough."

So she went up to the oven and took out one loaf after another. Then she walked on farther and came to an apple tree laden with fruit.

"Shake me! Shake me!" begged the tree, "for my apples are all ripe!"

So she shook the tree till the apples fell down like rain, gathered them all together in a heap, and went on farther.

At last she came to a cottage with an old woman standing

at the door. The old woman had such very large teeth that the girl was frightened and started to run away.

But the old woman called her back, saying, "What are you afraid of, my child? Come and stay with me. If you will keep my house neat and clean, then I will take good care of you, but you must be sure to make my bed well, and shake it very hard, so that all the feathers in my mattress fly, because then it snows on earth. I am Old Mother Frost."

As the old woman spoke so kindly to her, the girl took courage and agreed to work for her, and since she always shook the mattress so thoroughly that the feathers blew down like flakes of snow, her life was a happy one, and there were no harsh words, and she had roast meat and apple pie every day.

She stayed with the old woman for quite a long time; but one day, without knowing why, she felt homesick, and although she was a thousand times better off with Mother Frost than she was at home, she still longed to go. So she told Mother Frost that she wished to go home, and the old woman replied, "I can see you want to go home, and since you have helped me so faithfully and well, I will help you to get home again myself."

Then she took her by the hand and led her to a big door, which she opened, and, when the girl was under it, a huge shower of gold fell down and a great deal of it stuck to her, so that she was covered from top to toe with gold.

"That is for all your hard work," said the old woman, "and here is your spindle that fell into the well."

Then the door

was closed, and the girl found herself back up on the earth, not far from her mother's house; and as she came into the courtyard, the rooster called out,

"Cock-a-doodle-doo!

Our golden maid's come home again."

She went into the house, and because she was covered with gold, she was welcomed with open arms.

She told her story and when her stepmother heard how she had come by these great riches, she wished her ugly, lazy daughter to try her luck. So she ordered her to sit down by the well and spin.

The lazy daughter pricked her finger by running a thorn into it and smeared the blood all over the spindle. Then she threw the spindle into the well and jumped in after it. Like her stepsister, she came to the beautiful meadow and walked along the same path. When she arrived at the oven the bread called out, "Take us out, take us out, or we shall be burned. We have been baked long enough."

But she answered, "Do you really think I'm going to make myself hot and dirty because of you?" and walked on.

Soon she came to the apple tree, which called out, "Shake me! Shake me! My apples are all quite ripe."

But she answered, "I'm not coming any closer. You will all fall on my head," and she went on farther.

73

When she came to Old Mother Frost's house she was not afraid of the teeth, because she had been warned about them, and she too agreed to work for the old woman.

The first day she worked very hard and obeyed Mother Frost in all she said, because she kept thinking about the gold that would be hers. But on the second day she began to be lazy, and on the third even lazier until, in the end, she refused to get up at all. She did not make the beds either, and so the feathers in Mother Frost's mattress did not fly. The old woman got so fed up with her that she said she could go home, which pleased the lazy girl very much. For she thought, now the shower of gold will come.

The old woman led her to the door, but when she was beneath it, instead of gold, a tubful of tar was poured over her. "You get what you deserve," said Old Mother Frost, and shut the door on her.

Then home came Lazybones, covered with tar from top to toe, and when the rooster saw her, he crowed,

"Cock-a-doodle doo!

Your dirty daughter's come home again."

But the tar stuck to her, and as long as she lived, never, never came off again.

SLEEPING BEAUTY

Once upon a time there lived a king and queen who had no children, which made them very sad. One day, as the queen was walking down by the river, a little fish suddenly popped its head out of the water and said, "Do not be sad any more, for soon you will have a daughter."

What the little fish had promised did indeed come true, and the queen had a little girl who was so beautiful that the king was never tired of looking at her. He decided to hold a great feast to celebrate the birth of his daughter. So he invited not only his family, friends, and neighbors, but also all the fairies, so that they would shower kind and good blessings on his little princess.

Now there were thirteen fairies in his kingdom, and since he had only twelve golden dishes for them to eat out of, he had to leave one of the fairies without an invitation. The others came, and when the feast was over they all gave their best gifts to the little princess. One gave her virtue, another beauty, another riches, and so on till she had all that was excellent in the world. When eleven had finished blessing her, the thirteenth fairy, who was very angry because she had not been invited, suddenly came flying in, determined to take her revenge.

"When the king's daughter is fifteen," she cried out in a loud, menacing voice, "she will prick her finger on a spindle and fall down dead!" And then she left as suddenly as she had arrived.

Then the twelfth, who had not yet given her gift, came forward and said that she could not stop the bad wish from coming true, but that she could soften it. She declared that the king's daughter would not die, but instead would fall fast asleep for a hundred years.

The king desperately hoped to save his dear child from the evil wish and ordered that all the spindles in the kingdom should be found and destroyed at once. Meanwhile all the good fairies' gifts came true; for the princess was so beautiful and well-behaved, and kind and friendly that everyone who knew her loved her.

Now it so happened that on the very day she was fifteen years old, the king and queen were not at home and the princess was left all alone in the palace. So she wandered around by herself, looking in all the rooms till at last she came to an old tower. She climbed the narrow staircase and came to a little door with a golden key in the lock. When she turned the key the door sprang open, and there sat an old lady spinning away very busily.

The princess, of course, had never seen a spinning wheel, so she came closer and said, "How prettily that little thing turns around!" Then she took hold of the spindle and tried to spin. But as soon as she touched it, she pricked her finger and at once fell down lifeless on the ground.

She was not dead, however, but had only fallen into a deep sleep. The king and the queen, who had just come home, immediately fell asleep too; and so did their court, and the horses in the stables, and the dogs in the yard, and the pigeons on the rooftops, and the flies on the walls. Even the fire on the hearth stopped blazing and went to sleep; and the meat stopped roasting; and the cook, who was about to give the kitchen boy a box on the ear for something he had done wrong, let him go, and they both fell asleep; and so everything and everyone in the palace stood still and slept soundly.

A large hedge of thorns soon grew around the palace. Every year it became higher and thicker, until at last the whole palace was surrounded and hidden, so that not even the chimneys could be seen. But a rumor went through all the land about the beautiful sleeping Rosebud (for that was the princess's name), and from time to time daring princes came and tried to break through the thicket into the palace. But this they could never do, because the thorny bushes caught hold of them, and there they stuck fast and died miserably.

After many, many years a brave young prince came into that land. An old man told him the story of the thicket of thorns, and how a beautiful palace stood behind it in which a very beautiful princess, named Rosebud, lay sleeping along with all her court. He told, too, how he had heard from his grandfather that many, many princes had come and had tried to break through the thicket, but had become entangled in the cruel thorns and perished.

But the young prince said, "I am not afraid. I will go and see this lovely sleeping beauty."

The old man tried to stop him, but he would not listen.

Now that very day the hundred years were over, and as the prince came to the thicket there was not a thorn to be seen, but only masses of large and beautiful flowering shrubs. As he approached they parted to let him through and then closed after him like a solid hedge.

The brave prince came to the palace, and there in the court he saw the dogs asleep, and the horses in the stables, and on the roof the pigeons fast asleep with their heads under their wings. When he entered the great hall, he saw to his amazement the flies sleeping on the walls, and the cook holding up her hand as if she was about to box the kitchen boy's ears, and the maid sitting with a black hen in her hand ready to be plucked.

The prince went on farther, and all was so still and silent that he could hear every breath he drew. At last he came to the old tower and opened the door of the little room where Rosebud was. There she lay fast asleep. She looked so beautiful and peaceful that he could not take his eyes off her. Gently he stooped down and gave her a kiss.

The moment he kissed her, Rosebud opened her eyes and smiled at him with joy. As they went out of the tower and walked down the narrow staircase together, holding hands, the king and queen and all the court woke up and they gazed around at each other with great wonder. Then the horses got up and shook themselves, and the dogs jumped around and barked. The pigeons took their heads from under their wings and flew away into the forest; the flies on the walls started buzzing again, the fire in the kitchen blazed up and cooked the meat, the cook gave the kitchen boy such a box on his ear that he started yelling, and the maid went back to plucking the black hen.

The brave prince and Rosebud, the sleeping beauty, were married and lived happily together for the rest of their days.

THE FISHERMAN AND HIS WIFE

There was once a fisherman who lived with his wife in a little cold, damp hut, close by the sea. The fisherman went out fishing all day and every day. One morning, as he sat on the shore with his rod, looking at the sparkling water and watching his line, all of a sudden it was dragged away deep under the sea, and when he drew it up he pulled a great fish out of the water.

To the fisherman's amazement, the creature spoke to him: "Please don't kill me! I am not a real fish but an enchanted prince. Please put me back in the water and let me go."

"Oh!" said the fisherman. "Don't worry! I don't want to have anything to do with a fish that can talk, so you can swim away whenever you like."

Then he carefully unhooked it and put it back

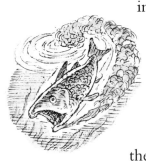 into the water, and the fish dived straight to the bottom of the sea, leaving a long streak of blood behind him.

When the fisherman went home to his wife in the little cold, damp hut, he told her how he had caught a great fish and how it had told him it was an enchanted prince, and that when he heard it talking he had let it go again.

"Didn't you ask it for anything?" said the wife.

"No," said the fisherman, "what should I ask for?"

"Well, really!" said the wife. "You know how miserable we are in this little cold, damp hut so go back and tell the fish we want a cozy cottage!"

The fisherman did not want to go but his wife went on and on at him so in the end he went back down to the sea, and when he got there the water looked all yellow and green. And he stood at the water's edge and said,

"Oh fish, great fish!
Come here to me, I pray
And grant my wife her wish
Before the end of the day."

Then the fish came swimming to him from the bottom of the sea and said, "Well, what does she want?"

"Ah!" answered the fisherman. "My wife says that when I caught you, I ought to have asked you for something before I let you go again: she does not like living in our little cold, damp hut, and wants a cozy cottage."

"Go home, then," said the fish, "she is in the cottage already."

So the man went home and saw his wife standing at the door of a cottage.

"Come in, come in," she said; "isn't this much better than the hut?"

And she showed him a sitting room and a bedroom and a kitchen; and a little garden behind the cottage with all sorts of flowers and fruits, and a courtyard full of ducks and chickens.

"Well!" said the fisherman. "How happy we will be now!"

"We'll see," said his wife.

Everything went well for a week or two, but then the fisherman's wife said, "Husband, this cottage is much too small and so is the courtyard, and so is the garden. I should like to live in a large stone castle, so go to the fish again and tell him to give us a castle."

"Wife," said the fisherman, "I don't like to go to him again, for perhaps he will be angry, and besides I am very happy with this cottage."

"Nonsense!" said the wife. "He will be glad to do it! So go along and try."

The fisherman went down to the sea again, but his heart was very heavy. The sea looked blue and gloomy, though it was quite calm, and he went close to it and said,

> "Oh fish, great fish!
> Come here to me, I pray
> And grant my wife her wish
> Before the end of the day."

"Well, what does she want now?" said the fish.

"I'm afraid," said the fisherman sadly, "she wants to live in a large stone castle."

"Go home, then," said the fish. "She is standing at the door of it already."

So away went the fisherman and found his wife standing at the gates of a great castle.

"Look!" she said. "Isn't this grand?"

The two of them went into the castle and found a great many servants there, and the rooms all

richly furnished and full of chairs and tables made of gold. Behind the castle was a garden and a forest half a mile long, full of sheep, and goats, and hares, and deer; and in the courtyard were stables and cowhouses.

"Well!" said the fisherman. "How happily we'll live in this beautiful castle for the rest of our lives."

"Perhaps," said the wife, "but let's sleep on it before we make up our minds." So they went to bed.

But the very next morning, when the fisherman's wife woke up she jogged him with her elbow and said, "Get up, husband, and stir yourself, for I must be king of all the land."

"Wife, wife," said the fisherman, "how can you be king? The fish cannot make you a king."

"Husband," she said, "don't say another word! Just go and ask him, for I will be king!"

So the fisherman went down to the sea once more, most upset to think that his wife should want to be king. The water was a dark gray color and covered with foam as he cried out,

"Oh fish, great fish!
Come here to me, I pray
And grant my wife her wish
Before the end of the day."

"Well," said the fish, "what does she want now?"

"Alas!" said the fisherman. "She wants to be king."

"Go home," said the fish. "She is king already."

Then the fisherman went home, and as he came close to the castle he saw a troop of soldiers and

heard the sound of drums and trumpets. Then he saw his wife sitting on a throne of gold and diamonds, with a golden crown on her head, and six beautiful ladies-in-waiting at her side.

"Well, wife," said the fisherman, "are you king?"

"Yes," said she, "I am king."

And when he had looked at her for a long time, he said, "Ah, wife! What a fine thing it is to be king! Now we shall never have anything more to wish for."

"We'll see," she said. "Never is a long time. I am king, it is true, but I am already getting tired of it, and I think I should like to be emperor."

"Oh wife!" groaned the fisherman. "Why do you wish to be emperor?"

"Husband," she said, "just go to the fish and say I will be emperor."

"Ah, wife!" replied the fisherman. "The fish cannot make you an emperor, and I don't like to ask for such a thing."

"I am king," said his wife, "and you are my slave, so go at once!"

So the fisherman had to go, but he muttered uneasily as he went along, "This will come to no good. It is too much to ask, the fish will be tired at last, and then we shall be sorry for what we have done."

He soon arrived at the sea, and the water was quite black and muddy, and a mighty whirlwind blew over it, but he went to the shore and said,

"Oh fish, great fish!
Come here to me, I pray
And grant my wife her wish
Before the end of the day."

"Now what does she want?" said the fish.

"We-ell," sighed the fisherman, "now she wants to be emperor."

"Go home," said the fish, "she is emperor already."

So he went home again, and as he came near he saw his wife sitting on a very tall throne with a very tall crown on her head, and on each side of her stood her guards and servants in a row, each one smaller than the other, from the tallest giant down to a little dwarf no bigger than my finger, and kneeling in front of her were all the princes and dukes of her empire.

The fisherman went up to her and said, "Wife, are you emperor?"

"Yes," she said, "I am emperor."

"Ah!" said the man, as he gazed upon her. "What a fine thing it is to be emperor!"

"Perhaps," said the wife, "I will think about it."

Then they went to bed, but the fisherman's wife could not sleep all night for thinking what she would be next. At last morning came, and the sun rose.

Aha! she thought as she looked at it through the window, I am emperor but I can't stop the sun from rising.

At this she was very angry, and she woke up her husband and said, "Husband, go to the fish and tell him I want to be lord of the sun and moon."

The fisherman was half asleep, but the thought shocked him so much, that he fell out of bed.

"Oh, wife!" he said. "That is God's work, can't you be content to be emperor?"

"No," she said, "I am very annoyed and cannot

bear to see the sun and moon rise without my permission. Go to the fish at once."

So the fisherman went, trembling with fear, and as he was going down to the shore a dreadful storm arose, so that the trees and the rocks shook. The skies grew black, lightning flashed, and thunder rolled; and in the sea great black waves reared up like mountains with a white crown of foam on them; and the fisherman said,

"Oh fish, great fish!
Come here to me, I pray
And grant my wife her wish
Before the end of the day."

"What does she want now?" said the fish.

"Ah!" said the fisherman. "Now she wants to be lord of the sun and moon."

"Go home," said the fish, "go home to your little cold, damp hut again!"

And there they live to this very day.

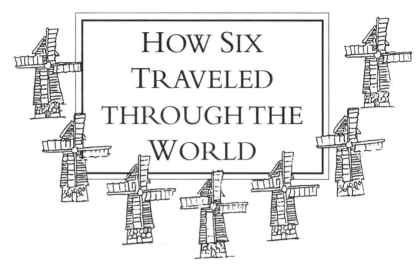

How Six
Traveled
Through the
World

There was once a soldier who had fought very bravely in a long war, but when it was over he was paid only three pennies for his services.

"That is not very fair!" he declared. "Perhaps if I find the right people, I will be able to make the king give me the treasures of the whole kingdom."

Feeling very angry he strode into a forest, where he found a man who had just uprooted six trees, as if they were straw. The soldier asked the man if he would be his servant and travel with him.

"Yes," replied the man, "but let me first take this bundle of firewood home to my mother." Then he picked up one of the trees, wound it around the other five, and carried the whole bundle on his shoulder. He soon came back and said to his master, "Well! The two of us will surely travel well enough through the world!"

They had not gone far before they met a hunter who was kneeling on one knee, getting ready to take aim with his gun.

"What are you going to shoot?" asked the soldier.

"The left eye of a fly sitting on the branch of an oak tree two miles from here," said the huntsman.

"In that case," said the soldier, "come with me, for if we three are together we will surely get on well in the world."

The huntsman agreed to go with him, and soon they arrived at seven windmills, whose sails were going around at a rattling pace, although there was no wind and not a leaf stirring.

"I wonder what drives these mills, for there is no breeze!" said the soldier, and they went on, but they had not gone more than two miles when they saw a man sitting in a tree, pressing on one nostril with a finger while he blew out of the other.

"What on earth are you doing up there?" asked the soldier.

"Didn't you see seven windmills two miles from here?" said the man. "I'm blowing on them to make the sails go around."

"In that case, come with me," said the soldier, "because if four people like us travel together, we are sure to get on very well in the world."

So the blower got up and went with him, and

before long they met another man standing on one leg, with the other leg unbuckled and lying by his side. The soldier said to him, "You have done this, no doubt, to rest yourself?"

"Yes," replied the man. "I am a runner, and I have unbuckled one of my legs so I can't run too quickly, for when I wear both I go as fast as a bird can fly."

"Well, then, come with me," said the soldier, "because five such fellows as we are will be sure to get on very well in the world."

The five heroes went on together and soon met a man who had a hat on over one ear. "Where are your manners?" said the soldier. "Don't wear your hat on one side like that; you look like an idiot!"

"I dare not straighten it," replied the man, "for if I do, there will be such a sharp frost that all the birds in the sky will freeze and fall down dead to the ground."

"Then come with me," said the soldier, "for it will be strange indeed if six fellows like us cannot travel quickly and easily through the world."

Then the six new companions went into a city where the king had promised that whoever ran a race with his daughter and won should marry her, but if he lost the race he would lose his head.

The soldier asked the king if his servant could run for him.

"Yes," said the king, "but if he loses then you must die as well."

"Of course," promised the soldier and then he told his runner to buckle on his other leg and to be sure of winning.

The runner and the princess were each given a cup and told to bring back water from a distant spring. They set off together, but the princess had run only a little way before the runner, in a puff of wind, was quite out of sight. He soon came to the spring, filled his cup, and turned back again, but had not gone very far before he began to feel tired, so he put his cup down again and lay down to take a nap. He made his pillow out of a horse's skull lying on the ground. Because his pillow was so hard, he thought he would easily wake up.

Meanwhile the princess, who was a better runner than many of the men at court, had arrived at the spring and was returning with her cup of water, when she saw the runner lying asleep. With great joy she emptied his cup and then ran on faster than ever.

All would now have been lost, but luckily the huntsman was standing at the top of the castle, looking out with his sharp eyes. When he saw the princess was winning the race, he loaded his gun and shot the horse's skull right from under the runner's head without hurting him in the least. The runner woke up at once, and leaping to his feet, he found his cup empty and the princess far ahead of him. However, he did not lose courage, but ran back to the spring, filled his cup again, and still got back ten minutes earlier than the princess.

The king and his daughter were annoyed that an ordinary soldier should win the prize, and so they plotted together how to get rid of him and his companions. Then the king called the six travelers

together and said, "You must now eat, drink, and be merry," and he led them to a room with a floor of iron, doors of iron, and windows guarded with iron bars. In the room was a table laid with delicious food. The king invited them to enter the room and enjoy a good meal, and as soon as they were inside he locked and bolted all the doors. He sent for the cook and ordered him to keep a fire lit beneath the room till the iron was red-hot. The cook did as he was told, and the six companions soon began to feel very warm.

At first they thought it was the hot food, but as it kept getting hotter and hotter, they tried to leave the room and found the doors and windows were locked. Then they realized that the king was up to no good and was trying to suffocate them.

"But he shall not succeed!" cried the man with the crooked hat. "I will call up such a bitter frost that this fire will go out," and he set about straightening his hat. Immediately such a frost fell that all the heat disappeared, and even the food on the dishes began to freeze.

When two hours had gone by the king was sure the six must be dead. He ordered the door to be opened and went in. But as soon as the door was opened, there stood all six alive and well and asking to come out to warm themselves, for the room had been so cold that all the food was frozen solid!

The king went down to the cook in a rage and scolded him and asked why he had not obeyed his instructions.

"There's nothing wrong with my fire!" declared the cook.

The king saw how fierce it was and went off to think up another way to get rid of his visitors. He sent for the soldier and said, "If I give you as much money as you like will you not marry my daughter?"

"Well, my lord king," replied the soldier, "just give me as much as my servant can carry, and you are welcome to keep your daughter."

This answer pleased the king very much, and the soldier said that he would come and fetch the money in fourteen days. During that time he collected all the tailors in the kingdom together, and made them sew him a huge sack. As soon as it was ready, the strong man, who had uprooted the trees, took the sack on his shoulder and carried it to the king.

When the king saw him, he said, "What a powerful fellow he must be, carrying this great sack upon his shoulders!" and began to worry about how much gold would fill it up.

He sent, first of all, for a ton of gold that needed sixteen ordinary men to carry it, but the strong man picked it up with one hand, shoved it into the sack and said, "Why don't you bring more at a time? This hardly covers the bottom of the sack."

Then little by little the king sent for all his treasures, but they did not even fill half the sack.

"Bring more, more!" said the strong man. "These are just crumbs." Then the king had to send for seven thousand wagons laden with gold, and all these the strong man piled into his sack—

gold, wagons, oxen, and all. But it still wasn't full, and only when everything and anything that they could find was put in, did the strong man say, "Well, I must make the best of a bad job and, anyway, if the sack is not quite full, it is much easier to tie up!" Then he hoisted it on his back and went off with his companions.

When the king saw this one man taking away all the riches of his kingdom, he got into a tremendous rage and ordered his army to go after the six men, and at all costs to bring back the strong man with the sack.

So two whole regiments chased after them at once and shouted out to them, "You are our prisoners! Lay down the sack of gold or you will be blown to pieces!"

"What are you saying?" asked the blower. "You will make us prisoners? But first you shall dance in the air!" And he closed one nostril with a finger and with the other he blew the two regiments high up into the sky, so that one flew over the hills on the right side and the other on the left.

One soldier begged for mercy: he had nine wounds and was a brave fellow who did not deserve to die, so the blower sent after him a gentle puff that blew him back to the king with a message that however many soldiers he sent, all of them would be blown into the air like the first group.

When the king heard this message he said, "Ohh! Let the fellows go! They must possess some kind of magic!" So the six companions took home all the wealth of that kingdom and lived contentedly for the rest of their days.

LITTLE RED-CAP

There was once a dear little girl who was loved by everyone who set eyes on her, and most of all by her grandmother who loved her so much that she could never do enough for her.

The grandmother had given the little girl a red velvet cap. It fitted her perfectly and she would never wear anything else. So she was named Little Red-Cap.

One day her mother said to her, "Come, Little Red-Cap, take this piece of meat and this bottle of wine to your grandmother; she is ill and weak, and they will do her good. Take them now before she gets up, but look where you're going and do not run, in case you fall and break the bottle, and then your grandmother will get nothing. When you go into her room, don't forget to say 'Good morning,'

103

and don't go peeking in all the corners."

"I will be very careful and do everything as you say," promised Red-Cap, and kissed her mother good-bye.

The grandmother lived far away in the forest, half an hour's walk from the village, and soon after Little Red-Cap entered the woods she met a wolf. She did not know what a wicked animal he was, and so she was not at all afraid.

"Good morning, Little Red-Cap," the wolf said.

"Good morning to you, wolf," said Little Red-Cap.

"And where are you going so early?" asked the wolf.

"To my grandmother's," said Little Red-Cap.

"And what have you got in your basket?" said the wolf.

"Good meat and wine," said Little Red-Cap, "for my grandmother, who is ill and weak."

"And where does your grandmother live?" asked the wolf.

"A little way farther into the forest," said Little Red-Cap, "her cottage stands under three great oak trees and near it are some hazelnut bushes, which make it easy to find."

The wolf said to himself, what a juicy, tender mouthful she will make! Much tastier than the old woman! I must be cunning if I want to snap them both up . . .

So he drew closer to Little Red-Cap and said, "Just look at the beautiful flowers growing all around you! You're not even looking at them! You walk along so solemnly as if you were going to school. I don't believe you can even hear how sweetly the birds are singing!"

Little Red-Cap looked around her and when she saw the sunbeams dancing through the trees, and what lovely flowers were blooming at her very feet, she thought, if I pick my grandmother a big bunch she will be so pleased. It is still very early so I've got plenty of time. And she ran from the path deeper and deeper into the forest looking for more and more flowers.

But the wolf ran straight to the grandmother's house and knocked on the door.

"Who's there?" asked the old lady.

"Only Little Red-Cap, bringing you some good meat and wine: please open the door," replied the wolf.

"Lift up the latch," cried the grandmother. "I'm too weak to get up."

So the wolf lifted the latch, and the door flew open. Without a word he jumped on the bed and gobbled up the poor old lady. Then he put on her clothes and tied her nightcap over his head, got into the bed, and pulled the blankets up to his chin.

All this time Red-Cap had still been gathering flowers and when she had picked as many as she could carry, she hurried to the cottage. She was very surprised to see the door wide open, and as soon as she came into the room she began to feel there was something wrong.

In a gentle voice she said, "Good morning, dear grandmother," but there was no answer, so she went up to the bed and there lay her grandmother with her nightcap pulled down over her eyes, looking very ferocious.

"Oh, grandmother," said Little Red-Cap, "what big ears you have!"

"All the better to hear you with," came the reply.

"And what big eyes you have!"

"All the better to see you with."

"And what big hands you have!"

"All the better to touch you with."

"And, grandmother, what big teeth you have!"

"All the better to eat you with," came the answer, and before the words were out of his mouth, the wolf leaped out of the bed and gobbled up poor Little Red-Cap.

Then he lay down again in the bed and soon fell fast asleep. He began to snore very loudly. A huntsman passing by overheard him, and thought, how loudly the old woman is snoring today! I'd better go in and see if she is all right.

So he went into the cottage, and when he came to the bed he saw the wolf lying in it.

"What are you doing here, you old rascal?" said the huntsman. "I've been after you for a very long time!"

And he killed the wolf with a single blow. Suddenly he guessed where the grandmother might be. He snipped open the wolf's stomach and out she crept with Little Red-Cap.

Little Red-Cap gave her grandmother the good meat and wine, which soon brought roses to her cheeks. The huntsman took Little Red-Cap home and she promised her mother that she would never, never wander from the path in the forest again.

THE TABLE, THE DONKEY, AND THE STICK

Long, long ago there lived a tailor who had three sons, but only one goat, who had to have good food every day to give them all plenty of milk. The sons took turns taking the goat to the meadow. One morning, for a change, the eldest son took the goat into the churchyard where the finest grass grew and let her frisk around till the evening.

When it was time to go home he said to the goat, "Have you had enough to eat?"

The goat replied,

> "I am satisfied, quite;
> No more can I bite."

"Then come home," said the boy and, catching hold of the rope, he led her to the stall and tied her up.

"Now," said the tailor, "has the goat had enough food?"

"Yes," replied his son, "she has eaten all she can."

But his father wanted to see for himself. So he went into the stall, stroked the goat, and asked her whether she had had enough to eat, to which the goat replied,

> "How should I be satisfied?
> I jumped from here to there all day
> And never ate a bite!"

"What's this I hear?" cried the tailor, and he ran to his son and said, "Oh, you bad boy! You said the goat had had enough to eat, and then you brought her home hungry!" Then he took a whip down from the wall and chased his son out of the house in a rage.

The next morning it was the second son's turn, and he picked out a place in the garden hedge, where some very fine herbs grew, which the goat happily gobbled up. When it was time to go home the boy first asked the goat if she had had enough to eat, and

she answered as before,

"I am satisfied, quite;
No more can I bite."

"Then come home," said the boy, and he drove the goat to her stall and tied her up fast.

Soon after, the old tailor asked, "Has the goat had her usual food?"

"Oh, yes!" answered his son. "She ate up all the herbs."

But the tailor wanted to see for himself, so he went into the stall and asked the goat whether she had had enough. But the animal replied,

"How should I be satisfied?
All day I jumped around the hedge,
And never ate a bite!"

"The naughty scamp!" exclaimed the tailor. "To let such a good animal starve!" He ran indoors and chased his second son out of the house with his whip.

It was now the third son's turn, and of course he wanted to make a better job of it than his brothers. So he found some bushes full of beautifully tender leaves and let the goat eat every single one of them. In the evening, when he wished to go home, he asked the goat the same question as the others had done and received the same answer,

"I am satisfied, quite;
No more can I bite."

So then he led her home and tied her up in the

stall. When his father came in and asked if the goat had eaten her fill of good food, the boy said that she had.

But the old tailor wanted to see for himself, and then the naughty goat lied to him, as she had done before, and said,

> "How should I be satisfied?
> All day I jumped around the bush,
> And never ate a bite!"

"Oh!" cried the tailor in a rage. "All my sons are scoundrels! This one is just as careless and forgetful as his brothers." And he rushed into the house and whipped his youngest son so soundly that the poor boy ran away.

The old tailor was now left alone with his goat, and the following morning he went to the stall and stroked her, saying, "Come, my dear little one! I will lead you myself into the meadow."

He took the rope and brought the goat to a luscious patch of clover, and let her feed to her heart's content.

When evening came he asked the goat, as his sons had done before, whether she had had enough to eat, and she replied,

> "I am satisfied, quite;
> No more can I bite."

So he led her home and tied her up in the stall, but before he left her, he turned around and asked once more, "Are you sure you've had enough to eat?"

The spiteful goat answered in the same way as before,

> "How should I be satisfied?
> All day I jumped around the clover,
> And never ate a bite."

The tailor was dumbfounded and realized at once that he had driven away his three sons for no good reason.

"Wait a minute, you ungrateful beast!" he shouted. "It's not enough just to send you away, I will punish you so that you never dare to show yourself among honest tailors."

Then he hurried off to fetch his razor and

shaved the goat's head as bare as the palm of his hand. This gave the poor goat such a fright that she ran off as fast as her legs would carry her.

When the old man sat down again in his house he felt so sad and lonely that he would have given anything to have his three sons back again, but no one knew where they had gone.

The eldest, in fact, had gone to work for a carpenter. He worked so well and cheerfully that when he left the carpenter gave him a table, which looked quite plain and was made of ordinary wood. But it had one special thing about it: if its owner stood in front of it and said, "Table, set yourself," the good table was at once covered with a fine cloth, and plates, and knives and forks, and dishes of roast meat and plum pudding appeared on it, and a great glass filled with red wine to cheer anyone's heart.

The young man thought, I will have enough here to last a lifetime. And he went off happily all over the world, never worrying if an inn was good or bad, or if there was food there in plenty or not.

More often than not he stayed in the fields or woods and whenever he felt like it he would take the table off his back, stand in front of it, and say, "Table, set yourself!" And then all the food he could possibly wish to eat or drink would magically appear before him.

At last he decided to go home to his father, because he felt sure he could not still be angry with him. He thought he would live very comfortably with his father and his wonderful table. It so happened that on his journey home he came to an inn one evening, which was full of people. They made him welcome and invited him to come in and eat with them.

But the young man said, "Thank you kindly but I would be happier if you would be my guests."

Everyone laughed and thought he was joking, but he put his wooden table down in the middle of the room and said, "Table, set yourself," and in the twinkling of an eye the table set itself with meats that made their mouths water.

"Help yourselves, good friends," said the young man; and the guests did not wait to be asked twice, but quickly sat down and ate. But they did wonder how it was that when any dish became empty, another full one instantly took its place.

The landlord of the inn, who stood in a corner looking on, thought to himself, I could make good use of a table like that, but he said nothing.

The young man and his companions sat making merry till late at night, but at last they went to bed, and the young man carefully pushed his wishing table up against the wall before going to sleep.

The landlord, however, could not get to sleep. Suddenly he remembered that there was an old table in his attic, so he fetched it and put it in the place of the wishing table.

The next morning the young man paid for his night's lodging and placed the table on his back without noticing that it had been changed and went on his way. By midday he had reached his father's house and was welcomed with joy.

"Now, my dear son," said the old man, "what have you learned out there in the world?"

"I have become a carpenter, father," said the young man.

"Excellent!" said his father. "But what have you brought home with you from your travels?"

"The best thing I have brought," said the young man, "is this table."

The father looked at it carefully and said, "You have been made a fool of. It is nothing but an old, worthless table."

"But, father!" interrupted his son. "When I stand in front of it and say, 'Table, set yourself,' it is at once covered with the tastiest meats and wine. Just invite your friends over and you'll soon see what a fine meal they will get."

As soon as the guests arrived he placed his table in the middle of the room and called out to it to set itself. But the table did not budge and remained as empty as any other table that does not understand when it is spoken to. The poor young man at once realized that the table had been changed over, and he was ashamed to stand there looking like a fool and a liar before his father's guests. They laughed at him and had to go home without anything to eat or drink. So the old tailor took up his mending again and stitched away as fast as ever, and the poor young man had to go and work for another carpenter.

Meanwhile the second son had been learning his trade working for a miller. When it was time for him to leave, the miller said to him, "Because you have worked so hard for me, I'm giving you this donkey, which has a wonderful gift, even though it can't pull a wagon or carry a sack on its back."

"What is it good for then?" asked the young man.

"It spits out gold," replied the miller. "All you have to do is call out 'Bricklebrit!' then the good beast will pour out gold coins like hail."

That is a very fine thing, thought the young man, and he thanked the miller and went off on his travels. Whenever he needed money he had only to say "Bricklebrit" to his donkey and it rained down shiny gold pieces. Wherever he went, only the best was good enough for him because he always had a full purse.

When he had seen quite a bit of the world, he thought he would go and visit his father who could not possibly still be angry with him. Besides, since he was bringing a gold-making donkey with him, he would surely be very pleased to see him.

It so happened that he came to the very same inn where his brother's table had been changed over. As he came up, leading his donkey, the landlord offered to tie it up, but the young man said to him, "Thank you kindly, but I will lead my gray beast myself into the stable and tie him up, for I must know exactly where he is."

The landlord was puzzled, and he thought that a

man who looked after his own donkey would not spend much money. But when the young man put his hand into his pocket and took out two pieces of gold and gave them to him, asking him to serve the best food he could, the landlord began to be interested. He quickly fetched the best food and drink he could lay his hands on.

When he had finished his meal, the young man asked how much he owed, and the landlord, who wanted to get as much money out of him as he could, said that he owed him two gold pieces. The young man felt in his pocket, but his money had run out, so he said, "Wait a minute and I'll go and fetch some more gold," and, taking the tablecloth with him, he went out.

The landlord did not know what to think; but, being greedy, he crept out after the young man and peeked through a hole in the stable wall. He saw the young man spread the cloth beneath the donkey and then call out "Bricklebrit!" and in a flash the don- key began to spit out gold, as if rain were falling.

"Heavens above!" exclaimed the landlord. "That is not a bad sort of purse!"

The young man paid his bill and soon after lay down to sleep, but in the middle of the night the landlord slipped into the stable and led away the goldmaker and tied up a different donkey in its place.

Early next morning, the young man went off with the donkey thinking it was his own, and at midday he arrived home. His father was overjoyed to see him again.

"What have you learned out there in the world?" he asked his son.

"I have become a miller," was the reply.

"And what have you brought home with you from your wanderings?" asked the old tailor.

"Nothing but a donkey," said his son.

"Oh, there are plenty of those around; it would have been better to bring back a goat," said the old man.

"Yes," replied the son, "but this is no ordinary donkey! Because when I say 'Bricklebrit!' it spits out gold everywhere. Just call your friends, and I will make them all rich in the twinkling of an eye."

"Well," exclaimed the tailor, "that would please me very much. Then I would not need to use my needle anymore," and he ran off to call all his friends together.

When they had all gathered around, the young miller told them to make a circle and, spreading out a cloth, he brought the donkey into the middle of the room.

"Now, watch this!" he said to them and called out "Bricklebrit!" but not a single gold piece fell from the donkey's mouth. The young man saw that he had been tricked, and he had to apologize to the guests, who went home as poor as they came. So the old tailor had to take to his needle again, and the young man had to find himself another job.

Meanwhile the third brother had gone to a thatcher to learn his trade. While he was there, his brothers sent him a message telling him how badly things had gone with them, and how the landlord had robbed them of their wishing gifts on their way home. When the time came for him to leave, his master gave him a sack, saying, "There's a stick in there."

"I will take the sack readily, because it may come in useful," said the young man. "But what is the stick for? It only makes the sack heavier to carry."

"What's it for?" said the thatcher. "I will tell you. If anyone does you any harm you have only to say, 'Stick, out of the sack!' and instantly the stick will jump out and dance around on the person's back so that they will not be able to move so much as a finger for at least a week, and what's more, it will not stop till you say, 'Stick, get back into the sack.'"

The young man thanked the thatcher, hung the sack over his shoulders, and set off for home.

One evening he arrived at the inn where his brothers had been robbed and, laying his knapsack on the table, he began to talk of all the wonderful things to be seen in the world.

"Yes," he said, "I've heard of a table that sets itself with food, and a golden donkey, and such things—all very good in their way, but they are next to nothing compared with the treasure that I carry with me in my sack."

The landlord pricked up his ears at once. "What on earth can it be?" he said to himself. "The sack must be full of precious stones, and I must get hold of them somehow, for all good things come in threes."

As soon as it was bedtime, the young man stretched himself out on a bench and laid his sack down for a pillow. When he seemed to be in a deep sleep the landlord crept softly up to him and began to pull very gently and cautiously at the sack to see if he could pull it out and put another one in its place. But the young thatcher had been waiting for him to do this and, just as the landlord gave a good tug, he cried out, "Stick, out of the sack with you!" Immediately out it jumped and thumped around on the landlord's back and ribs with all its might.

The landlord began to cry for mercy, but the louder he cried the faster and fiercer the stick beat time on his back, until at last he fell to the ground.

Then the young thatcher said, "If you do not give up the table that sets itself with fine food and the donkey that spits out gold, my stick will beat you all over again."

"No, no!" cried the landlord in a weak voice. "I will give them back with pleasure, but just make your horrible hobgoblin get back into his sack."

"All right," replied the young thatcher, "but you'd better keep your promise," and he ordered the stick to get back into the sack.

The following morning the young man left the inn with the table and the donkey. When he got home, his father was overjoyed to see him and asked what he had learned in the big wide world.

"Dear father," he replied, "I have become a thatcher."

"That's a difficult business," said his father, "but what have you brought back with you from your travels?"

"A precious stick," replied the son, "a stick in this sack."

"What!" exclaimed the old man. "A stick! Whatever for? Why, you can cut one from any tree, anywhere!"

"But not a stick like this," said his son. "For if I say, 'Stick! Come out of the sack,' it instantly jumps out and gives anyone who would hurt me such a thumping that he falls to the ground, begging for mercy. Look! Thanks to this stick I have the wonderful table back again and the gold-making donkey that the thieving landlord stole from my brothers! Now, call them both home and invite all your friends, and I will not only give them plenty to eat and drink but pockets full of money."

The old tailor did not really believe him, but all the same he did as he was told. Then the young thatcher spread a tablecloth in the middle of the room and led in the donkey, saying to his brother, "Now, speak to him."

The young miller called out "Bricklebrit!" and in a flash, gold pieces were dropping down on the floor in a pelting shower, which did not stop until everyone had so much money that they could not carry any more.

After this the table was fetched in, and the

young carpenter said, "Table, set yourself," and it was at once covered with the tastiest food. Then they feasted on a meal the likes of which the tailor had never had in his house before, and the whole company stayed there till late at night as merry as can be.

The next day the tailor put away his needle and thread for good and lived happily ever after with his three sons.

But now I must tell you what happened to the goat, whose fault it was that the three brothers were driven away. She was so ashamed of her bald head that she ran into a fox's hole and hid herself.

When the fox came home he saw a pair of great eyes looking at him in the darkness, which so frightened him that he ran away and came face to face with a bear, who saw how terrified the fox was and said to him, "What is the matter, Brother Fox?"

"Oh!" said the fox. "There's a horrible beast in my hole, who glared at me with the most fiery eyes."

"Oh! We'll soon chase it out," said the bear going up to the hole and peeking in. But as soon as he saw the fiery eyes, he also turned tail and took flight from the terrible beast.

On his way he met a bee who said, "Why do you look so frightened, Mr. Bear, have you lost your sweet wife?"

"No," whimpered the bear, "there's a great horrible beast lying down in Brother Fox's house, glaring at us with such fearful eyes that we are afraid to chase him out."

"Well, Mr. Bear," said the bee, "I am sorry for you; you never take much notice of me, but still I believe I can help you."

So she flew into the fox's hole and settled on the goat's shining bald head and stung her so dreadfully that the poor animal sprang up and ran madly off, but where to nobody knows to this day.

THE BRAVE LITTLE TAILOR

One summer's morning a tailor was sitting on his bench by the window in very good spirits, sewing away with all his might when he saw a peasant woman coming up the street calling out, "Jam! Jam! Good jam for sale!"

The tailor liked the sound of that so he stuck his cheerful little head out of the window and called out, "Here, my good woman, just bring all your jam up here!"

The woman climbed the three steps up to the tailor's house with her heavy basket and began to unpack all the pots of jam.

The tailor inspected each one, held them up to the light one by one, sniffed at them, and at last said, "Your jam seems to me to be very good, so weigh me out four ounces, my good woman, I don't mind even if you make it a quarter of a pound."

The woman, who had been expecting the tailor to buy much more jam than that, gave him what he wished and went away grumbling, very much dissatisfied.

"Now!" exclaimed the tailor, "God bless this jam, and give me health and strength!" and he took the bread out of the cupboard, cut himself a huge slice (the size of the whole loaf), and spread the jam on it. "That will taste good," he said, "but, before I have a bite, I'll just finish this vest." So he put the bread down near him and went on sewing away, making larger and larger stitches all the time in his excitement.

Meanwhile the tempting smell of the jam was rising up to the ceiling, where flies were sitting in great numbers, and soon a huge swarm of them had settled on the bread.

"Hey!" exclaimed the tailor. "Hang on a minute! Who invited you?" He flapped his hands at the uninvited guests, but the flies, not understanding his language, would not be driven off and soon came back in even greater numbers than before.

This made the little tailor so furious that in his rage he snatched up a piece of cloth and took an almighty swipe at them. When he lifted the cloth he counted no less than seven flies lying dead before him with outstretched legs. "What a fellow you are!" he said to himself, marveling at his own bravery, "the whole town shall know about this." And he quickly cut himself out a belt, hemmed it, and then sewed on it in large letters "Seven At One Blow!"

"Ah," he said, "not just this city but the whole world shall know about this!" and his heart fluttered with joy, like a lamb's tail.

The little tailor put the belt on and got ready to go out into the wide world, because he now felt that his workshop was too small for his brave deeds. Before he set out, however, he looked around to see if there was anything he could take with him; but all he found was an old cheese, which he pocketed, and then he noticed a bird that had got stuck in a bush by the front door, so he caught it, and put that in his pocket too. Then he set out bravely on his travels, and since he was fit and healthy, he did not feel at all tired.

His road led him up a hill, and when he got to

the top he found a great giant calmly sitting there.

The little tailor went boldly up to the giant and said, "Good day, comrade, sitting there with the whole world stretched out below you. I am also going there to try my luck. How about coming with me?"

The giant looked down scornfully at the little tailor and said, "You good-for-nothing! You wretched, pathetic little man!"

"That may be," replied the tailor, "but look! This will tell you what sort of a man I am," and, unbuttoning his coat, he showed the giant his belt. The giant read "Seven At One Blow" and thinking that the tailor had killed seven men he was secretly quite impressed, but nevertheless he decided to test him out first. He picked up a stone and squeezed it in his hand so hard that water dripped out of it.

"Now you do that too," said the giant to the tailor, "that is if you have enough strength."

"Is that all?" said the tailor. "Why, that's child's play to me." And he put his hand into his pocket, took out the cheese and squeezed it till the whey ran out of it, and said, "Now, I'd say my squeeze was better than yours."

The giant did not know what to say—he could not believe that the little man was so strong. He picked up another stone and threw it so high that it could scarcely be seen with the naked eye, saying, "There, little man, now you do the same as me."

"Well done," said the tailor, "but in the end your stone did fall again to the ground. I will throw one up that will never come back!"

And he dipped into his pocket, took out the bird, and threw it into the air. The bird, overjoyed to be free again, flew away, and of course did not come back.

"So what do you think of that comrade?" asked the tailor.

"You can certainly throw well," replied the giant, "but now let's see if you are strong enough to carry something out of the ordinary." And the giant led the little tailor to a huge oak tree lying on the ground and said, "Will you help me to carry this tree out of the forest?"

"Of course!" replied the tailor. "You take the trunk on your shoulder, and I will lift all the branches and leafy twigs, which are the heaviest parts of the tree, and carry them."

The giant heaved the trunk onto his shoulder, but the tailor quietly sat down on a branch, so that the giant, who was unable to look around, was

forced to carry not only the whole tree but the tailor as well. The tailor laughed to himself at the trick and began to whistle a merry song as if the carrying of trees were child's play.

The giant staggered along with his heavy burden until he could go no farther. Then he stopped and shouted out, "Can you hear me? I'm letting the tree fall."

The tailor quickly jumped down and put his arms around the tree, as if he had been carrying it all the time. "You're such a big fellow," he said to the giant, "can't you really carry this tree by yourself?"

They journeyed on together in silence till they

came to a cherry tree. The giant seized the top of the tree where the ripest fruits hung and, bending it down, gave it to the tailor to hold, telling him to eat. But of course the tailor was much too weak to hold the tree down, and when the giant let go the tree flew up into the air and the tailor with it. He landed unhurt and the giant said, "What happened? Aren't you strong enough to hold on to a small branch?"

"Of course I am," replied the

tailor. "You don't really think that that was difficult for a man who has killed seven at one blow? I sprang with the tree because I saw some hunters shooting down there in the bushes, so you had better spring after me if you can."

The giant tried to, but could not jump over the tree and got stuck in the branches, so once more the tailor came out of things the better of the two.

Then the giant said, "Since you are such a brave little fellow, why don't you come and spend the night at my house with me and some friends of mine?"

"Thanks," said the tailor. "I'd like that very much." And he followed the giant into a cave where two other giants were sitting by the fire, each gnawing on a whole roast sheep. The tailor sat down and said to himself, "Ah! This is the life! Much more like the world than my workshop!"

The giant showed him a bed where he could lie down and sleep. But the bed was much too big for him, so he crept out of it and curled up in a corner.

In the middle of the night, when the giant thought the tailor would be in a deep sleep, he got up, and taking a great iron bar, brought it down on the bed at one stroke and was sure that was the end of the little tailor.

At the crack of dawn the giants went off into the forest, quite forgetting the tailor, when before long, he caught up with them as cheerful and merry as ever. The giants were terrified and, fearing he would kill them all with his extraordinary strength, they ran away as fast as their legs would carry them.

The tailor journeyed on, always following his nose, until he came into the courtyard of a royal palace. Since he felt rather tired he lay down on the grass and went to sleep. While he was lying there the people came and had a good look at him and read on his belt, "Seven At One Blow."

"Ah," they said, "what is this great warrior doing here in time of peace? He must be some mighty hero." So they went and told the king, thinking that if a war suddenly broke out, here was a man who should not be parted with at any price. The king sent a messenger to the tailor to ask if he would stay with them.

The messenger waited at the sleeper's side till he yawned and stretched and opened his eyes, and then he gave him the king's message.

"Why that's the only reason that I came here," said the little tailor. Then he was led away and treated with great honor and given a fine house to live in.

The king's knights, however, became more and more jealous of the tailor. "What will happen," they said to one another, "if we go to battle with him and he strikes seven at one blow? There will be nothing left for us to do."

In their rage they all went to the king and said, "We are not prepared to keep company with a man who kills seven at one blow."

The king had no desire to lose all his faithful knights for the sake of one little man and wished that he had never seen the tailor. But he did not dare to send him away, because he was afraid that the tailor would kill him and put himself upon the throne.

He thought and thought until at last he had a very good idea. He sent for the tailor and said, "Since you are such a great hero, I want you to do me one favor: in a certain forest in my kingdom there live two giants who have given us every kind of trouble for many years, but no one dares to go near them for fear of losing his life. If you kill both these giants I will give you my only daughter in marriage and half my kingdom, and I will send a hundred knights with you to help you."

"Oh, yes," he said to the king, "I will soon deal with these two giants. A hundred horsemen are not necessary for that purpose—he who kills seven at one blow need not fear two."

Ah! This is just the thing for a man like me! thought the tailor happily to himself. You don't get offered a beautiful princess and half a kingdom every day of the week!

The little tailor set out, followed by the hundred knights, but when they came to the edge of the forest he said, "Now all of you stay here; I would rather meet these giants alone." Then he crept into the forest, peered around him, and after a while he saw the two giants lying asleep under a tree, snoring so loudly that the branches above them shook violently. The tailor, full of courage, filled both his pockets with stones and climbed up the tree. He crawled along a branch till he was just above the sleepers, and then he let one stone after another fall onto the chest of one of them.

The giant did not budge for a while, until at last, half asleep, he pushed his companion and said, "Stop hitting me!"

"You must be dreaming," said the other giant, "I didn't hit you." And they lay down again.

When they had gone back to sleep the tailor threw a stone down on the other giant.

"What's going on?" he roared. "What are you hitting me for?"

"I didn't touch you—you must be dreaming," replied the first giant. They bickered for a few minutes, but they soon fell asleep again. Then the tailor chose the biggest stone of all and threw it with all his force onto the first giant's chest.

"That's it!" yelled the giant and, springing up like a madman, he fell upon the other giant, and the two of them began to fight each other so fiercely that they rooted up trees and beat one another about until they both fell down dead.

The tailor jumped down and went to the horsemen and said, "The deed is done, but it was a hard job, for they even uprooted trees to defend themselves with. Still, all that is nothing to a man like me who has killed seven at one blow."

"And you are not wounded?" they asked.

"Good heavens, no! They haven't touched a hair of my head," said the little man. The knights simply did not believe him, till they found the giants lying dead and the uprooted trees around them.

The tailor now asked the king for his reward, but the king did not want to keep his promise.

"Before I give you my daughter and half my kingdom," he said, "you must do one more thing. There is a unicorn running wild in the forest, and I want you to catch it."

"Ha! I'm even less frightened of a unicorn than I was of two giants! Seven at one blow! That's my motto," said the tailor.

Then he fetched a rope and an ax and went off to the forest. He had not been searching long when the unicorn appeared and started to rush at him there and then.

"Softly, softly!" whispered the little tailor, "that is not so easily done." He waited till the animal was almost on him, then he sprang nimbly behind a tree. The unicorn, rushing with all its force against the tree, rammed its horn so deeply into the trunk that it could not draw it out again, and so it was caught. The tailor leaped out from behind the tree, put the rope around the unicorn's neck, cut the

horn out of the tree with his ax, and led the animal before the king.

The king, however, still would not give the tailor the promised reward. He insisted that before the wedding the tailor should catch a wild boar that did much harm.

"With pleasure," was the tailor's reply, "it is mere child's play."

As soon as the boar saw the tailor it ran at him with gaping mouth and glistening teeth and tried to throw him to the ground; but in a trice our flying hero sprang into a little chapel nearby and

out again through a window on the other side. The boar ran after him, but the tailor just skipped around and shut the door behind it. There the raging boar was caught, because it was much too heavy to jump out of the window.

The tailor then asked the king to come and see his prisoner with his own eyes, and now the king was obliged, whether he liked it or not, to keep his promise and give the tailor his daughter and half his kingdom. The wedding was celebrated with great splendor, though with little rejoicing, and the little tailor was made a prince.

Soon afterward the princess heard her husband talking in his sleep, saying, "Boy, make me a vest, and stitch up these trousers, or I will whip you with my tape measure!" Then she realized what her husband really was, and in the morning she told her father and begged him to rescue her from her husband, who was nothing but a poor tailor.

The king said, "There, there! Leave your bedroom door open tonight, and when he is asleep my servants will enter, tie him up, and take him away to a ship, which shall carry him far away from here."

The princess was delighted with this plan; but the king's armor bearer, who had overheard everything, went to the new prince and warned him of the plot.

"Leave this to me," said the little tailor. That night when his wife thought he was asleep she got up, opened the door, and lay down again. The tailor, however, was only pretending to be asleep, and began to call out in a loud voice, "Boy, make me this vest, and stitch up these trousers, or I will whip you with my tape measure! Seven have I killed with one blow, two giants have I slain, a

unicorn have I led captive, and a wild boar have I caught, so why should I be afraid of those men now standing outside my room?"

When the men heard what the tailor was saying they were so frightened that they ran away as if ten giants were after them.

No one ever dared to send him away after that, and that's how the little tailor became a king and remained a king for the rest of his days.

RUMPELSTILTSKIN

There was once a poor miller who had a beautiful daughter. One day he had to go and speak to the king and, wanting to seem important, he told him that he had a daughter who could spin straw into gold.

The king was very fond of gold and thought to himself, now that is a skill that would please me very much. So he said to the miller, "If your daughter is as clever as that, bring her to the castle in the morning, and I will put her to the test."

As soon as she arrived the king led her into a room that was full of straw; and, pointing to a spinning wheel, he said "Now get to work, and if you have not spun this straw into gold by an early hour tomorrow, you must die."

With these words he shut the door and left the

151

girl all alone wondering how to save her life, for she had no idea how on earth straw might be spun into gold. She grew more and more desperate as time passed and began to cry.

All at once the door opened and in stepped a little man, who said, "Good evening, pretty one. Why are you crying so bitterly?"

"Ohh!" she sobbed, "because I'm supposed to spin this straw into gold, and I don't know how to do it."

The little man asked, "What will you give me if I spin it for you?"

"My necklace," said the girl.

The dwarf took the necklace, sat down in front of the spinning wheel, and whirr, whirr, whirr, three times around, and the bobbin was full. Then he set up another, and whirr, whirr, whirr, thrice around again, and a second bobbin was full, and so he went all night long, until all the straw was spun and the bobbins were full of gold.

At sunrise when the king came, he was astonished and delighted to see so much gold, but it did not make him less greedy. He led the girl into a still larger room full of straw and told her to spin all of it into gold during the night if she did not want to lose her life.

The poor girl again had no idea what to do, but while she was crying the door opened suddenly as before, and the dwarf appeared and asked her what she would give him in return for his help.

"The ring off my finger," she replied.

The little man took the ring and began to spin at once, and by the morning all the straw was changed to glistening gold.

The king was overcome with joy at the sight of it, but he was still not satisfied; and, leading the girl into another even larger room full of straw, he said, "If you spin all this during the night, you shall be my bride."

For, he thought to himself, a richer wife there would not be in all the world.

When the girl was left alone, the dwarf appeared again and asked her, for the third time, "What will you give me if I do this for you?"

"I have nothing left that I can give you," she replied.

"Then promise me your firstborn child if you become queen," he said.

The miller's daughter thought, who can tell if that will ever happen? And, having no idea how else to help herself out of her trouble, she promised the dwarf what he desired, and immediately he sat down and finished the spinning.

When morning came, and the king saw the huge heap of gold, he married the miller's pretty daughter and so she became queen.

About a year after the marriage, when she had forgotten all about the little dwarf, she brought a lovely child into the world. One day, soon after its birth, the queen was cradling her baby in her arms when suddenly that very same dwarf appeared before her. He demanded what she had promised him. The frightened queen offered him all the riches of the kingdom if only she could keep her child.

"No," answered the dwarf, "something human is dearer to me than all the wealth of the world."

The queen began to weep and groan so much that the dwarf felt sorry for her.

"I will give you three days to think it over," he said, "and if during that time you find out what my name is, you shall keep your child."

All night long the queen racked her brains for every name she could think of and sent a messenger far and wide through the land to collect any new names.

When the dwarf appeared the following morning, the queen was ready for him with a list of unusual names.

"Is it Caspar?" she said. "Or Melchior? Or Belschazzar?"

But at each name the little man said with glee, "No! That is not my name."

The second day the queen asked everyone for uncommon and curious names and asked the dwarf if he was called "Ribs-of-Beef," or "Sheepshank," or "Whalebone," but always he said, "No! That is not my name."

The third day the messenger came back and said, "I have not found a single name, but as I came to a high mountain at the edge of the forest, where the fox and the hare say good night to each other, I saw a little house there, and outside the door a fire was

burning, and around this fire a very strange little man was hopping around on one leg, and shouting,

> "Today I stew, and then I'll bake,
> Tomorrow I shall the queen's child take;
> How glad I am that nobody knows
> My name is RUMPELSTILTSKIN."

When the queen heard this she was overjoyed, for now she knew the dwarf's real name.

That afternoon, the dwarf appeared, grinning from ear to ear, so sure was he that today he would collect his prize. "Now, my lady queen," he said, "what is my name?"

First she said, "Are you called Conrad?"

"No."

"Are you called Hal?"

"No."

The queen paused for a moment. "Are you called *Rumpelstiltskin*?"

"A witch has told you! A witch has told you!" shrieked the little man, and he stamped his foot so hard that it went right through the floor. In a great rage he tugged and pulled at it so hard that it nearly came off in the struggle. Then he hopped away howling terribly, and from that day to this he has never been seen again.

TITLES IN THE TREASURY SERIES